I0606639

He'd just learned he had a daughter…only to discover she had been abducted…

"She's mine, isn't she? Abigail's mine. I have a daughter, have had a daughter for twelve years, and never knew it. Why didn't you tell me?"

"Because you were such a noble, upright young man. You would have immediately wanted to 'do the right thing by me' and insist on marrying me. That would have put you working in some factory in Fort Smith to support your family. You would have hated it. And you would have quickly resented me as the cause of your frustrations and ended up hating me. Our marriage would not have survived. Besides, my grandmother always told me if I ever got pregnant to never marry the father because it never worked out. Remember Andy and Sue, or even Rick and Jane, they were ahead of us in school? It didn't work for them. You needed college and the freedom to go there. I had a part of you with me. I knew I would always love you and your child."

"Oh, Marsha, how I love you!" he whispered, drawing her close. "I know now that's why I never married, because I've always loved you. And now, I have a daughter to love."

"No, no," she cried, pushing him away. "Abigail's missing, has been since late yesterday afternoon. We've been looking everywhere and haven't found her yet."

Chicago PD detective Colton Mitchell takes a nostalgic vacation back to his home town of Midland, Arkansas, expecting a simple vacation. But he's totally unprepared for what he finds when he gets there. Reuniting with his high-school sweetheart, he discovers that he has a daughter—but she's missing, another one of seven children who have disappeared from the sleepy, rural town over the past few years. Now Colton's in a race against time to save the daughter he never even knew he had and to rid the town of the evil that's been preying on their children…

In *Errant* by Mary Jane Bryan, Colton Mitchell is a Chicago cop who decides to take a trip down memory lane and head back to his old hometown for a visit. When Colton arrives, he runs into his old high school flame, whom he hasn't seen in nearly twelve years. As they talk and catch up on their lives since high school, Colton discovers to his joy that he has a daughter—one his old girlfriend never told him about until now. But as Colton rejoices at the unexpected turn of events, he learns, to his horror, that his twelve-year-old daughter is the latest in a string of young children who have disappeared from this small town, never to be seen again. Determined to find and rescue the little girl he never knew he had, Colton uncovers much more than he would ever have thought possible. The story is tense, fast-paced, and creative, with some wonderful characters. This one will have you continually on the edge of your seat. ~ *Taylor Jones, The Review Team of Taylor Jones & Regan Murphy*

Errant by Mary Jane Bryan is the story of a man who doesn't know what he has until he loses it—literally. Colton Mitchell never really got over Marsha, the girl he loved in high school. When he graduated and went away to college, he expected her to be waiting for him at home. But she suddenly moved to California and never answered any of his letters. Now, twelve years later, Colton is a cop in Chicago. He returns to his hometown on vacation and Marsha is there, distraught because her twelve-year-old daughter has been missing since the day before. Colton is stunned to learn that Marsha has a daughter, and even more stunned when he does the math and realizes that Marsha must have been three months pregnant with his child when he left for college and she never even told him. But any joy he feels at learning that he has a daughter is dampened by the horror of discovering that the girl is missing, likely abducted by whoever—or whatever—has been periodically stealing children from this small Arkansas town since 1957. *Errant* is well written, tense, heartwarming, and fast paced. It will hook you in from the very first paragraph and keep you reading all the way through. ~ *Regan Murphy, The Review Team of Taylor Jones & Regan Murphy*

ACKNOWLEDGMENTS

Thanks to all my family and friends for their support, patience, and understanding. My love to all of you.

Errant

A Mystery
by

Mary Jane Bryan

A Black Opal Books Publication

Errant:

1. Behaving wrongly.

2. Straying outside the proper path or bounds.

Prologue

The Delivery

1939:

This was going to be a hard delivery, she could tell.

The position of the baby was all wrong and, try as she had so far, it had not turned into the proper head-down angle. The mother was exhausted.

With every contraction, the mid-wife told the mother to push and push harder, but each time the woman had fallen back on the pillows, so exhausted she did not think she could push even one time more. She kept muttering something that sounded like "babies" to the mid-wife, but the mid-wife thought the mother was only delirious with her pain.

The midwife let her rest each time between contractions, hoping against hope that the baby would turn into the proper position with its head down into the delivery canal. She knew she was going to have to try to reach inside and turn the baby. She was grateful for small hands. These petite hands had delivered many babies around this community for many years now.

She was tired herself, not only tired because of age, but also tired of delivering all these babies. Why everyone thought only *she* could deliver one, she did not know. Oh, sure, she had started out years ago assisting the local country doctor, because these people had no way of getting to his office in the next town over, much less into the city to the hospital, to have their babies. But she had proved so skilled and invaluable that the women had stopped calling for the doctor and had only started calling for her to come.

They even thought that it was good luck to have her come, that if Granny delivered the baby, then it would have a fortunate life. Where that thought came from, she did not know, either, as well as why they only called for her.

But she came, every time she was called. Yes, she might groan inwardly whenever she heard that some young, even middle-aged woman was pregnant, but she knew she would always go when called.

If the truth were known, although she was growing weary, she started enjoying the reputation she was acquiring around the countryside. Not only had the women in this small town called for her for all her adult life, but the news had spread to other communities in this rural part of Arkansas.

Whenever she heard a horse or buggy coming down the lane, she started gathering up her materials. It was best if they came by buggy, for she had transportation to the home and back about a week later, if all went well. If not, she had her own mule that she saddled up and accompanied the man—for it was usually the husband who came for her—back to the wife or daughter that required her services.

And all always seemed to go well. That's how her reputation grew and her fame for easy deliveries spread so rapidly. If the baby happened to be in the wrong position, as now, she always managed to move it rapidly and gently into the delivery position without too much damage to the mother.

She had never lost a baby or a mother. These women were of good country stock and bore their babies well. Good clean living and hard work made them strong and able to deliver well.

This woman's husband was in the next room, pacing back and forth, back and forth. This was their first child, so it was understandable, but she still wished he would sit down and be quiet.

She reached up inside the mother with the next strong push and gently moved the baby around. But it didn't feel right, somehow not the same shape as usual.

The baby came, head first as it should, and then with one big effort, its whole body came out, still connected to the mother by the cord.

Then it opened its mouth to let out a cry.

The midwife nearly dropped the baby.

The husband rushed in, uninvited, before she cleaned or prepared the baby. The mother had fainted from the exhaustive effort of delivery, but she was okay.

The husband took one look, gasped, and backed out of the room. The shock was too much for him.

Granny took the small, squirming bundle to the open, low window and placed it on the ground outside. She would dispose of it later.

She forgot about the husband as she and her assistant began cleaning the mother.

But, wait!

There *was* another?

Chapter 1

Colton

June 1976:

If they had one, Colton could have been the "poster-child" for his suburban Chicago police department. He was a tough, big-city cop. He lived and breathed his job "by the book." He didn't take any guff off anyone and didn't give any, either. His partner and other officers knew he had good instincts and often used those in the field.

The public knew him as a fair man and greeted him as such.

He was simply a no-nonsense type of guy.

That's why, when he started having thoughts of going back to visit his old hometown, the small town in western Arkansas where he had grown up, he wondered about himself.

Now, why did he think about going there? He hadn't thought about the old home place for many, many years now.

Colton graduated. His high school sweetheart went to California for a visit right after graduation and stayed there. She never answered any of his letters or calls. He left for college in the fall and, at the same time, his folks moved to the nearest big city. None of them had looked back, at least not as far as he knew.

The closest thoughts he had ever had of the old town was when Mary Lou Remick—now Johnson—tracked him down and told him all about his tenth high school reunion and then kept bugging him about coming, even after he told her he had no plans to come. She was so enthusiastic about all the planned events and had made it her personal task to get everyone to attend. She only stopped calling when she reached him the morning of the Friday night event and realized he was still in Chicago and had no time to make it to Arkansas. She was so disappointed.

He moved on immediately.

But, now? Why were all these thoughts returning repeatedly, almost begging him to get back there?

There really was nothing there then—they closed the

school when Colton's class graduated. They were the last class. His mom told him in one call they had torn the old building down and now any students, the very few that seemed to be left in the town, were bussed to the next small town over, but still a bigger town than this one.

So, what was there to go back to in his old hometown? A few abandoned buildings and fallen-down homes? He was just not a nostalgic type of person.

Yet, something kept nagging at him and wouldn't let go.

☙❧

Colton put his pen down, having signed his last report for the day. He pushed his chair back, lifting his arms high above his head, stretching.

"Another round of paperwork done," he said to himself. He put his right hand on the back of his neck, rubbing it.

He was tired.

He had watched these men for months and had finally made a drug bust today.

Now, if they'll just receive jail-time convictions, I won't feel I've wasted my time, he thought.

Hearing raised voices, he looked around, seeing several of his fellow officers at the bulletin board.

"Hey, Mitchell," one of them called to him. "You finished pushing that pencil yet?"

"Just done," Colton replied.

"Then get yourself over here. Captain's just put up the vacation calendar and your name's on top of the list to choose your dates. If you'll come do it, the rest of us can get our names down and beat the night shift."

"Gotcha," said another man, grinning.

"Did it again!"

The night shift had complained bitterly for years that it never got a chance to pick out their vacation times first. It seemed like the day shift always got the best dates.

Colton got up from his desk, taking his report to the captain's "IN" box on the way to the bulletin board.

There were several groans and "you would" as he put his name and brackets on the Wednesday before the Fourth of July weekend. This gave him an extra day off.

"Sorry, guys! These dates have been on my mind for a while now. Don't know why."

Being single, he had always chosen "time off" times carefully. He would plan his time so that the men and women with families would have the choice times during the summer, when their children were out of school and they all could enjoy a family vacation together. Choosing "The Fourth" was not like him.

"Want to trade?" one man asked. "The kids are in camp those two weeks and Alicia and I thought we'd get away by ourselves somewhere. What do you say?"

He hesitated, seriously considering trading with his friend, but something kept him from agreeing.

"Sorry, I just need these days," he said, shaking my head. "I'd do it, but…" He shrugged.

As he turned away, several others went back to their desks, also.

"Got any exciting plans?" one man asked. "If you need those certain days, what's so important about them, aside from the fact you get an extra day, of course?"

"I'm not sure," Colton said. "I've been thinking lately about a trip back to my old hometown. You know, where I grew up as a kid."

"And where's that?"

"Place called Midland," he replied.

"Texas?"

He shook his head. "Nothing as glamorous as Midland, Texas, I'm afraid. No, it's a small, very small, town in western Arkansas, south of Fort Smith. Ever heard of Fort Smith?"

"Nope," several voices said.

"I have," one said.

"Really?"

"Sure," the man replied. "I'm a western novel fan, read about a Judge Parker. He was from Fort Smith. He commissioned and sent marshals over into Oklahoma, then just known as Indian Territory. They were the only law there. The 'Hanging Judge,' they called him. Seems it was an important western town at one time. Farthermost town west and all that. Not really a big town, though, is it?"

"About seventy thousand, is all," Colton replied. "And Midland's much smaller."

"How small?" his partner asked. "You've never really talked about your childhood or where you're from, you know."

"Promise not to laugh," Colton said, grinning, looking around at the men and two women still there from the day shift.

This was the time of day he liked best. It wasn't quitting time yet, but it was close enough that no one would be starting anything new. In a few minutes, the members of the night shift would start drifting in. He had no particular time to leave, or come, for that matter. As a detective, he sometimes didn't come into the office at all, depending on the assignment. During the investigation that had just ended this morning, he had been out in the field, working undercover, more than in the office.

But when Colton had a report to do, he tried to be here at this time. There was a certain camaraderie about this group that bound them not only as police officers, but also as friends.

He had eaten in many of their homes, gone to watch their kids play ball, and even suffered through several blind dates that a few of the well-meaning wives had set up for him.

But no one promised not to laugh. He really had not expected them to. This group always had a good sense of humor to laugh or make fun of any situation.

"You asked for it," he said. "Here goes. There was a total of eight hundred and thirty-two persons living in Midland when I was a boy!"

Several laughs broke out.

One man had been taking a sip of coffee when Colton said the number. He spit the coffee out, spraying it over his desk.

"You gotta be kidding!" several said, at the same time.

"What did you do for fun in a place like that?" one asked, grinning.

"I don't know about now, of course," he replied. "That was many years ago. I did graduate high school there, twelve years ago." Colton smiled. "Bet you didn't know I was that old, did you?"

"Ha! Ha!"

"You that young?" one asked.

They all liked him. He was a good cop, a good detective. He had a natural intuition, a sixth sense, about his work that served him well during investigations. He had saved several of their lives simply by shooting at the right time, stopping the perps, just "sensing" where they were.

"Seriously, Colton," said another, "what are you going back there for? You have an old girlfriend stashed away, or something?"

"I wish," Colton said. He shrugged, spreading his hands. "I'm really not sure why. Must be one of those old nostalgic things people feel sometimes. I started thinking about it a while back. Thought I'd look the old place over, see if any of my old buddies are still around, and then drive home slowly."

"Home" was a large city near Chicago, Illinois. When he had left Midland twelve years before to go to college to study law enforcement administration, he had no idea this was where he would be at age thirty. He had thought of returning to Arkansas, running for county sheriff, and being there the rest of his life.

But this city was as good as any other place and probably better than some. The city had been good to him.

"You've been a big city boy for so long now, you'll be bored in about five minutes, you know."

"Guess I'll just have to find that out for myself," he said, rising.

"Yep, time to go," another said.

"Here come the night rats," he said, referring to the night shift.

For several minutes, there was a shuffle and change of positions as they moved in and out of the room.

Brad, a good friend of Colton's, caught up with him as they started down the back steps to the parking lot.

"Hey, Colton," he asked, "are you serious about traveling down to Arkansas?"

Brad had invited him to go on vacation with the family before, and Colton had joined them several times, especially during the winter to ski in Vail, Colorado.

"Besides," his friend continued. "I never knew you were from Arkansas. You never seemed like you were from the 'real' country."

"I'm serious," Colton said. "And I honestly can't tell you why. The thought just came to me. That date just came to me, too, at the same time."

"Hey, you think something's going on? Some 'force' pulling you, or something? Maybe you'll go down there and enter *The Twilight Zone*."

Colton laughed. "I doubt it. I'm sure it's just like I said, a sudden attack of nostalgia to see the old home place."

As much of a friend as this man was, Colton was not about to tell him about the "visions" he had started having around the same time he started thinking of Midland.

No one had ever thought he was crazy.

He sure didn't want them to think so now.

Chapter 2

It

July 1957:

It was not aware that it was in the basement of a house. Indeed, it had no concept of a *house*. It only knew that it *was*. This awareness began when it was young but not yet strong enough to do anything for itself. For a long time one of the things above it had come down to feed it.

It sensed the moaning, creaking, and settling of the boards of the house. It recognized the drying out and neglect that set into the boards once the breath of humans was no longer around to keep the wood alive. It felt a type of sorrow for the boards, assuming that, as it had needed the humans for its life, the wood needed them for the same source of life.

It developed at a slow pace. A long time passed before it realized there were no more sounds above it, and that one of the things above him brought no more food. Now it fed only on bugs, mice, and other small animals that happened to come through a tiny hole in the base of the outside cellar door. Up to this point, they simply had appeared before it, seemingly willing to be its food. But these did not satisfy or supply its hunger for long.

It had never moved from this dank, cool place. It had no need to move when the human brought food to it.

Now, however, the hunger was so great it stirred.

Chapter 3

Colton Goes Home

*R*educe speed ahead, forty-five to thirty-five to twenty-five. Midland.

Colton slowed only slightly as he moved off the highway to turn left into Midland. A sign opposite the road indicated Midland to the left, Sugar Loaf Mountain to the right.

He remembered swimming and going on picnics to Sugar Loaf Mountain. Sometimes there had not even been enough room to park, if you arrived too late in the morning on weekends or holidays. He had enjoyed the large crowds, though, and that was probably why he enjoyed living in the big city now.

He turned to the left, and then he was entering his old hometown.

He turned slowly onto Main Street, Midland.

The first building he came to was the old general store, once advertising *GENERAL MERCHANDISE AND DRY GOODS* on its side. There were still traces of the letters, but perhaps you would recognize them only if you knew they were once there. It still had the front porch the length of the building, with wide, plate-glass windows. The double glass front door was still in place, down to the original hand-beveled glass.

The building was still in use. To Colton, the visible signs of life were the three rocking chairs spread across the front porch, two of them on either side of a half barrel with a checkerboard on top of it.

He wondered if any of the men in town still played. Then he wondered how many men actually still lived in this small town. It had such a still, unlived-in sense about it.

When he was a boy, as soon as one man got up— either because he was tired of checkers or probably had lost too many games—another was ready to take his place, hoping to defeat whoever was reigning champion of that day. There had been an unwritten rule: whoever won the most games that day got his evening mug of beer paid for by the others. So, a game was always in progress.

Of course, back then, there were still plenty of men in town to keep a game going.

The general store was a free-standing building and the next block started a row of businesses. Now it appeared that most of them had been closed up for years.

But he remembered what had occupied each space. The store on the corner, the one where the double doors faced the stop sign, had been the tobacco shop. He could see them in vivid, living color and felt people walking up and down the sidewalk, stopping to talk to each other, laughing.

At least that image came as a child. But then images came of people moving away, less and less people walking and laughing, and more and more people looking and talking in a very serious manner. Sometimes even in a very hushed manner.

His parents never allowed him to go in the tobacco shop. The proprietors then had more of a moral sense of responsibility than some did now. As a young boy, he made sure he parked his bicycle around the corner, down the side, off Main Street, so he could have every opportunity to amble past the open doors, taking slow, deep breaths.

The smell of the various tobaccos was heavenly to a boy who dreamed of smoking a pipe and wearing a fancy smoking jacket like the ones he saw on TV. That would make him rich, or that's how it appeared.

He could imagine the smells as he drove by.

Next to the tobacco shop had been the candy store. Mrs. Little also had a doll collection that attracted the girls. The candy store was his excuse to go past the to-bacco shop with its wonderful odors. To buy a nickel's worth of candy was all he needed to tease some girl and pull her pigtail. And there was always a girl in there, or so it seemed.

Mrs. Little would scold him and tell him to "shoo," but he always managed to hang around for a little while.

The third store was a beauty shop, Kate's Kut 'N Kurl. This was a new name to Colton. There were two cars parked out front.

The next storefront displayed a hand-painted "Crafts" on the window. Although there did appear to be a few items in the windows, the sign on the door read "closed."

Colton wondered if that meant this store wasn't open for business yet that day, since it was early, or if it were permanently closed.

Across the street had been the biggest grocery store in town. It closed many years ago. The old metal Coca-Cola machine was still on the front porch.

He remembered running across the street from the candy store, putting his other nickel in the slot, and pull-ing the glass bottle across and up. If no one else was around, he had a hard time opening, holding up the heavy lid, and sliding the Coca-Cola across and up at the same time.

But he would never forget the taste of those Cokes! Sometimes he only got a dime to spend so it was a real treat. He would nurse it as long as possible. There were times, instead of candy, he would buy a bag of peanuts, drink the Coca-Cola down a little, then empty the bag into the bottle. It was the best way to drink a Coke and eat peanuts.

Next to the grocery store was the newspaper office. By the looks of things, it had also long since closed. There was a time when no one went without reading *The Weekly.* He could picture his mother pouring over the gossip columns and "tsk-tsking" at some tidbit or other. Of course, the ladies who submitted the columns, even from the outlying communities, would never have admitted it was gossip, but rather items of interest to the community. Besides, didn't everyone like to see his or her name in print?

A newspaper stand containing the *Southwest Times-Record,* a Fort Smith paper, now stood on the sidewalk. Since there were so few businesses open in town, he realized why the local newspaper had stopped being published.

Colton's attention went back to the other side, to the feed store, which was still in business. Hoes, rakes, and shovels stuck up out of a barrel on the sidewalk. At least someone was still making a living here. The next block was barren, but the sidewalk and old fire hydrant were still there. The old town library building had long since gone.

Then he was through Main Street, turning right,

down between rows of houses. He used to live on Maple Street. Yes, the house was there but lived in by strangers, since his parents had sold it.

He pulled to a stop at the side of the street, reminiscing. He could almost see himself flying out of the front door, taking the steps two by two, running down the sidewalk, and then down the street, his dog beside him all the way, matching stride for stride, his tongue lolling out of his mouth, as if he were laughing, enjoying the romp.

After driving slowly up and down several streets, slowing to look at old friends' houses and the ballpark, he decided to go back to the general store. That's where he would find out what was happening in town.

Chapter 4

Little Annie

July 1957:

It started the day Little Annie Mercer disappeared. And although it started that day, nobody knew it started.

Little Annie Mercer was not little at all. Actually, she was an All-American tomboy, stocky and robust, and could put some of the boys to shame at baseball or just about anything else.

They named her "little" from birth, when she was named Annie after her mother. To distinguish between them, she became "Little Annie" while her mother was

"Big Annie." Like all nicknames, it had stuck through the years.

Little Annie played shortstop on the local boys baseball team, a position not readily sought after by girls of the day. Not only did most girls prefer to simply look pretty on the sidelines, most young men preferred them there.

But Little Annie was different. She had grown up as "one of the boys" and it seemed natural for her to be on the team.

So, when Annie told her mother she was on her way to ball practice, Big Annie merely nodded and told her to have a good time. Big Annie's soap opera was about to begin. Her concern was directed to her new TV program and not at Annie.

But then, there was nothing unusual about Annie heading out for ball practice. The field was only four blocks away. In fact, it was a normal day in the life of this sleepy little Arkansas town.

Only Annie never made it.

"Mom?" asked Little Annie, from the doorway.

"Yes, dear?" Big Annie answered, absentmindedly. She had knelt down in front of the TV set, adjusting the knobs. *As the World Turns* was coming on in a few minutes, and she couldn't wait to see what Bob and Lisa would do next. She had quickly become an ardent fan of Lisa shortly after the program began airing.

Little Annie knew better than to disturb her mother

while her favorite show was on. "Some of the guys are meeting down at the field for a little ball practice."

Big Annie glanced up, noting her daughter standing there, already dressed in her usual practice clothes, complete with cap. Little Annie held her ball glove in one hand and a bat in the other.

"Sure, run along, dear. Have a good time, okay?" Big Annie smiled. She loved her daughter, her only child, and had long since given up on the bows and frills. If being a "tomboy" was natural for Annie, then she let her be one.

"Thanks, Mom, see you later. Enjoy your show."

"Thanks," was the reply. Big Annie had already turned back to the TV. She did not turn around for a final look at her daughter.

Little Annie left the house humming the tune to "The Mickey Mouse Club." As she reached the street she was singing "M-I-C-K-E-Y M-0-U-S-E" out loud. Little Annie was a happy girl, content in her world of baseball and Mickey Mouse, and secure in the love of her parents.

Her house was in the middle of the block on Oak Street. At the corner of Oak and Elm, she turned left on Elm. Elm Street was on the edge of town. It circled the town and was the quickest way to the town's one and only baseball field. Also, using Elm meant you'd miss the Black's mean old dog, Buster, who lived farther down on Oak. He'd never actually bitten anyone, but no one got close enough to test him.

All in all, it was a beautiful, perfect summer day.

As Little Annie continued walking along Elm, where it started to curve, she started feeling funny. "Funny" was the first word that came to her mind. And she didn't mean "ha-ha" funny, but "strange" funny. She felt the tiny hairs on the back of her neck stand up with the feeling that someone was watching her.

She stopped, turned first one way and then the other, looking for someone, anyone who might be near.

She did not see anyone in the direction of Spenser's Lane when she looked that way, but as she turned back toward town, someone grabbed her from behind. Her baseball cap fell off and one of the barrettes holding her bangs back from her face fell to the ground.

Although Little Annie was strong for her age, she was no match for the strength that held her. A large hand on her mouth prevented her from screaming, and a large arm around her body, holding her arms to her sides, made struggling impossible.

The terror she felt made her faint.

She was not aware of being lifted off the ground. She stirred once as she was being carried along and her eyes fluttered open. For one fleeting second her mind became aware of where she was and she panicked.

"Spenser's Lane! I'm on Spenser's Lane!"

Just

Just don't

Just don't go

Just don't go down
Just don't go down Spenser's
Just don't go down Spenser's Lane
Just don't go down Spenser's Lane by yourself
EVER

Do
Do you
Do you hear
Do you hear me?

A bumblebee buzzed around her head and she tried to raise her right hand to swat it away, struggling as she did so. The one and only thing Little Annie was afraid of was a big, fat yellow-and-black striped bumblebee. She was unaware she knocked off her baseball cap. She lost consciousness again.

Then, for a split second, she again became aware of her surroundings and a horrible odor that made her gag. Her eyes opened wide. She had only seen this place once before, when a large group of adults and children had walked this way to swim at Number Six, the local swimming hole. The children had all groaned and squealed, while the adults tried to calm them.

"There is nothing to be afraid of," they said.

It was just an old, abandoned house, like others that occasionally dotted the countryside. Anyway, the adults had taken the children's hands and hurried past the place.

No, I can't be here, she thought, before, once again, she struggled feebly to free herself of her captor. She did not feel her neck snap to end her struggles.

As she was lifted through the house, the other barrette fell out of her hair. They were her favorite blue barrettes that she always wore to ball practice or ball games to keep her bangs off her forehead. The barrette hit the hard floor with a slight "clink" sound. It stayed where it landed.

Little Annie had no more thoughts.

Chapter 5

Old Man Ogden

June 1976:

Ogden was mumbling away to himself as Colton went through the door of the store. He paused for a minute, watching the old man. Ogden stared out into space, gesturing with one hand. The other hand held a roll-your-own cigarette.

Colton had stepped into the general store of his childhood. It was as if the store hadn't changed at all. This was his first stop in his old hometown and he was not disappointed. Old Man Ogden seemed to be sitting in the same chair, by the same old stove.

Colton approached the old man, who by now had seen him and had stopped talking, smoking his cigarette instead.

He is *the one, I know,* Ogden thought. *He's the one to do it, but does he know he's the one? That's the big question. 'Cause, if he don't listen and understand, then all is lost. After all, maybe he only came into the store for a pack of cigarettes, or something. Could be he'll just think I'm a crazy old fool, like everyone else does.*

Old Man Ogden willed Colton to understand. Because Ogden was getting older all the time and if someone didn't listen to him soon, it would just go on and on. Children would continue to disappear. But if someone would just listen to him and believe, it *could* be stopped.

The old man kept his eyes on Colton as he drew near.

"You Abe Mitchell's boy, hain't you?" the old man asked, studying Colton closely. "Hain't see you in years. Where'd you get off to?"

"After college I went to work near Chicago, Mr. Ogden," Colton answered, politely, with respect.

The old man smiled, showing several gaps where teeth had long since disappeared. "Remember me, do you, huh?" He seemed pleased.

Yes, Colton remembered him. He seemed old when Colton was a boy. Yet, here he was, still looking old, even older, if that were possible.

"Come back because Marsha Miller's little girl's

missing, have you? Poor little Abigail. Still, she hain't been the first and she won't be the last. Unless—"

The old man looked at Colton sharply his eyes clear, questioning.

But Colton wasn't paying attention to the look the old man was giving him. Marsha had a daughter! Marsha Miller had been Colton's girlfriend in high school. They had been inseparable until Colton had gone away to college and Marsha went to California to live with an aunt. He had written her many letters, but there had been no response. Then, a final one came from her, asking him to stop writing. He had, with a broken heart. But he didn't know she had a little girl.

Then it registered what the Old Man Ogden had said.

"She wasn't the first and won't be the last what?" Colton asked, knowing he'd just get Mr. Ogden started on one of his stories. But he was curious, all the same. He could find someone else later to sort the facts out for him, or so he thought.

The old man looked at him, squinting. "Let's see. What age you be now, young Mitchell?"

"Thirty," answered Colton, wondering what the old man was getting at.

Ogden nodded his head. "Thirty. That'd make you eleven when the first one disappeared."

Eleven! What an age! Fishing, baseball, Number Six—

Suddenly, something flashed in his mind. "Little Annie," he said, before he thought, or could stop himself. *Now, where did that name come from?* He hadn't thought of her in…how many years? Fifteen, maybe? Eighteen? Too many to remember. And why that name now?

"Ah, you do remember, don't you?" Ogden began. "Little Annie, who wasn't little at all, disappeared into thin air one day on her way to ball practice. Case never solved. Nary a clue found as to why, how, or where. But you remember Little Annie. Tomboy all the way. Could beat up all the teen-age boys and probably half the men in town as well. And she knew where to kick a man to mean business. Parents taught her never to talk to strangers or accept rides, just as all you were. So, what do you think would have happened if some man had stopped her? She'd have punched his lights out, that's what. Probably with the baseball bat she was carrying. But there she was, or wasn't, if you like. Just gone! And never heard from again."

"Big Annie was never the same after that. Blamed herself, but I don't know why. Little Annie was just going to ball practice, four blocks down, that's all. Did it a hundred times, if one." Old Man Ogden was going full steam, for sure. "Then, three years later, there was Lucy Killan. Went swimming, down to Number Six. Folks said she always went down Main to County Line, then to the hole. By herself she was. Then gone. Just like Little Annie three years before. Folks reckoned the same sicko, same psycho bastard got them both."

The old man paused, but not for long. "Then he waited three years again, just like them other two. You remember Kelly Baird? Just disappeared going swimming, just like Lucy. Eleven years old and pretty as a picture. You remember Kelly?"

Colton nodded. Yes, he remembered Kelly. Pretty, blonde, and a cheerleader. He also remembered Lucy, as Old Man Ogden had rattled on. But he had forgotten about them, as teen-agers did when they grew up and moved away. Or had he conveniently forgotten about them? Had he wanted to forget? Three children disappearing in nine years' time without a clue.

But what was Ogden saying now?

"...and Tommy, Sally, Bob, and Junie since then, making that, seven children in twenty years. *Children,* mind you. Never grown-ups. People saying it sounded like a sex sicko to them. Could be, I suppose, someone who gets his thrills and then lays low for several years before striking again. And to think it could be anyone. Just anyone here in Midland. Maybe my next door neighbor, maybe..."

Old Man Ogden's voice trailed off, and Colton thought maybe he'd talked himself out but he started up again.

The old man looked up at Colton. "But it's not, you know, it's not any *one* around here. There's something here, all right, taking our little children every three years, but it hain't human, hain't human at all."

Colton mentally agreed. Anyone who would kidnap children, doing who knows what to them and with them, probably burying them somewhere, certainly was less than human.

He thought he had seen everything and anything possible in the big city. He would never have dreamed that anything like this was happening in a small, rural Arkansas town.

His town.

That was what Colton thought the old man meant. He nodded to him and started toward the door.

"Nope, hain't human at all," the old man repeated.

Chapter 6

Marsha

Colton knew where he was heading. He was going to the home where Marsha had lived twelve years ago. He had practically lived at it while they were going steady.

Had it been twelve years? So long?

As he drove along, his memories of her were strong. They had been a really "hot" item the last two years of high school. Everyone had called them the "M and M's" because their last names were so much alike. Not only their names, but they got along so well. They had broken the relationship when he announced that he was going away to college. Sure, Marsha had cried when he left.

That was to be expected, but, as he remembered, not a whole lot.

In fact, it almost hurt his ego the way she carried on so little.

But the important thing now was to locate her and find out if her daughter really was missing. He needed to get the facts.

As he rounded the last corner to her house, a wave of nostalgia hit him. The street didn't appear to have changed at all. The thick hedgerow was still on the right, next to the sidewalk, shielding the Emerson's place from the public. They were that way. Next would be the Walkers, then Marsha's place, if, in fact, her parents still lived there. Colton hadn't even thought to ask Ogden where she lived.

Yes, the name on the mailbox was the same, and still in need of repainting.

Colton parked his car on the street, about halfway down from the house. If the mailbox had not had the name on it, he would still have suspected he was at the right place because of the number of cars around it. He had pulled up behind two other cars on the street.

Friends and family always liked to gather when things like this happened, listening to all the grieving details, watching how people "took" it. Whether these people helped in such situations was debatable. Probably not, but it made the well-meaning comforters feel good for some perverse reason.

He rang the doorbell, and it struck him that he had not even thought about what he was going to say to Marsha. Before he had time to think about it, though, the screen door opened and she stepped out.

Colton caught his breath! Here was the same Marsha he had left twelve years ago. Here was the same flaming red, gorgeous hair, cut now in a modern style. She was still slim and beautiful, hardly looking a day older, even with her red-rimmed eyes and tear-stained cheeks.

"Colton!" she breathed and was in his arms before he knew it.

Colton felt as if he had come home at last. She felt so right and wonderful in his arms. The last twelve years might never have been, the way he felt holding her, stroking her hair with one hand and her back with the other, as he used to do.

She started sobbing.

"Shh," Colton said, breathing in the scent of her hair, almost swaying with the thrill of the touch and smell of her. *This is why I haven't married all these years,* he thought. *I've never stopped loving her.* "Shh, it's all right, please don't cry," he begged her.

This was a different cry from when they parted long ago. This was a heart-wrenching cry that had nothing to do with him or his ego. In this cry was all the anguish of the knowledge of a daughter not returning home.

He held her for several long minutes, until she quieted down, and backed away from him.

"Oh, Colton, it's so good to see you." She sighed. "But why are you here? You couldn't possibly know about Abigail missing? We've been trying to keep it as quiet as possible."

"I didn't know when I first got into town this morning," he said. "My trip was simply nostalgic. One of those 'back-to-the-old-hometown-roots' sort of thing. I just had a sudden urge to come here, to see the old place again. I ran into Old Man Ogden at the general store and he recognized me. He asked if I'd come to town because of your daughter? Marsha, I'm sorry, but I didn't even know you had a daughter. When did you marry? Tell me what's been happening."

She had stopped sobbing and had stepped away from him and now she looked down, twisting her handkerchief around in her hands.

"Shall we go back twelve years?" she asked.

"Sure," he replied. "It's always good to start at the beginning."

He smiled, hoping to cheer her up, but she remained solemn.

"Let's sit on the swing," she said, turning toward the end of the porch.

Amazing, thought Colton. *This is the same porch swing we sat in then. It has the same narrow, green boards, the same rusty chain holding it to the ceiling. Wow, even the same squeaks as we sat down.*

He took her hands in his.

"When you left to go to college," she began, "I left to go live with my Aunt in California."

Colton nodded. That much he knew.

"She was wonderful in taking care of Abigail. Aunt Betty June and Uncle Jack had never had any children of their own, so they literally doted on Abigail, on us, really. Uncle Jack made enough money that my aunt stayed home and she took care of Abigail while I worked. Auntie never asked me to pay rent or buy groceries, but she felt it was good for me to work and to provide for Abigail's needs. Fortunately, I found a job that paid a good salary and had good benefits. We only moved back here about a year ago when Mom had a stroke. Dad was killed five years ago in a car accident in Fort Smith, and Mom's always had high blood pressure. Auntie said she'd help us with finances if we needed her."

Here, Marsha flashed a smile, which made Colton's heart skip a beat. That beautiful smile, But now only a fleeting one.

"Everyone should have an aunt like my Auntie June," she said.

"But your husband? Your marriage? What about them? When did you marry?" Colton asked.

She looked straight at him. "I've never been married," she whispered.

"But—your little girl—Abigail—" he began. "Wait! Just how old is Abigail?"

"Twelve."

"Twelve!" Colton exclaimed. "Twelve. When—when was she born?"

"February 11, 1965," Marsha replied. "That's why I went to live with Auntie in California, to have my baby. And Auntie never blamed me, or judged me, or 'preached' at me. She just simply took me in and loved me. She and Mom were as close as sisters could be and she would have done anything for her, and for me. There was never any question about giving up the baby. No matter what, I was going to keep her, or him, if that had been the case. Wait," she said. "I'll get you a photo."

Marsha got up, rocking the swing, and disappeared through the screen door.

"February, 1965." Colton's head was spinning. "Twelve!"

That meant Marsha had been about three months pregnant when they parted. But she'd never said anything to him, not a word!

No! Could it be? The thought that perhaps Abigail could be his daughter hit him so hard, he stood up, jerking the swing so violently it hit against the back of his knees.

When was that night? But it had only been one night. Graduation? They had been so happy, so much in love, and yes, they had gotten carried away that night. They'd gone farther than they had ever gone before. But could it have happened with only the one time?

Obviously, it could.

He was still standing, stunned with the realization that Abigail could be his, when Marsha came back, carrying a photo in a frame and also a photo album.

When Colton saw the photo of Abigail, he no longer doubted. Abigail looked just like he did at that age, only she was a girl. She looked like his mother had at that age. But would Marsha admit it to him? He only knew he had to find out.

"Marsha," he began, and something about the tone of his voice caused Marsha to look up at him, to where he was staring at her daughter's photo.

Blue eyes met his unwaveringly.

She's waiting for me to discover it, he thought. "She's mine, isn't she? Abigail's mine. I have a daughter, have had a daughter for twelve years, and never knew it. Why didn't you tell me?"

The anguish and longing in his voice brought tears to her eyes, but they never left his face.

"Because you were such a noble, upright young man. You would have immediately wanted to 'do the right thing by me' and insist on marrying me. That would have put you working in some factory in Fort Smith to support your family. You would have hated it. And you would have quickly resented me as the cause of your frustrations and ended up hating me. Our marriage would not have survived. Besides, my grandmother always told me if I ever got pregnant to never marry the father because it never worked out. Remember Andy and Sue, or even

Rick and Jane, they were ahead of us in school? It didn't work for them. You needed college and the freedom to go there. I had a part of you with me. I knew I would always love you and your child."

"Oh, Marsha, how I love you!" he whispered, drawing her close. "I know now that's why I never married, because I've always loved you. And now, I have a daughter to love."

"No, no," she cried, pushing him away. "Abigail's missing, has been since late yesterday afternoon. We've been looking everywhere and haven't found her yet."

Colton felt awful. Caught up in the emotion of discovering he had a daughter, he had forgotten she was missing. "What happened, where was she last seen?" he asked. "I'll do what I can to help find her. Maybe it's not too late."

Marsha let out a huge sigh. "She asked if she could go down to Number Six to swim. I asked her how many were going and she said 'everyone,' which I knew meant about six of her friends that were always with her and played together. She said she was meeting them about two blocks down, on the corner, so of course I let her go. I mean, how many times had she been swimming this summer? Dozens, at least. How many times did we go every summer?"

Colton nodded, understanding. But he felt a shudder, suddenly remembering one particular day when he was late, everyone else having gone ahead, and he had to walk to Number Six by himself. Without quite knowing why, it seemed important to know which way she went to get there.

"How did she get there?" he asked, urgently.

"Why, she rode her bike, of course," Marsha answered. "They all rode their bikes to Number Six."

"No, no, I mean which *way* did she go to get there? County Line Road or Spenser's Lane?"

"I'm really not sure. Could it have been Spenser's Lane?" Marsha exclaimed. "You've got to be kidding! Oh, no, I forgot you've been gone a lot of years. *Nobody* takes Spenser's Lane anymore! Unless you're several of the locals trying to hunt together and I've heard them complaining about never being able to find any game out that way. It's really overgrown now, not nearly big enough for a car. There is still a path, though, that some animals must take, or something. But the growth is so dense, it's too difficult to go through there. None of the children go that way that I know of. I heard years and years ago that no one used Spenser's Lane anymore, almost by silent knowledge of the people around here. Just something about it. Much too spooky. And don't forget that old house we all thought was haunted, the old Spenser House."

That was exactly what Colton was remembering, the old Spenser House and a time when a voice, loud and clear, told him to run for his life. And run he had, knowing his life was in danger…

သြသြ

1957:

Spenser's Lane was such that only one car could travel down it at a time. If two happened to meet, then one had to back all the way out or be at one of the rare places where it could pull over just far enough for the other to pass by.

Mostly, local youngsters used Spenser's Lane as a shortcut to Number Six, the favorite swimming and fishing hole for miles around.

That's where eleven-year-old Colton was headed today, with his fishing pole in one hand and his tackle box in another, a towel draped across it. He was alone, having had to finish extra chores before he could make the day his own. He hadn't been able to decide whether he wanted to fish or swim, so he had brought his fishing gear just in case. He knew if he didn't bring it, he'd probably start seeing big fish jumping and wish he'd taken it along.

He didn't like the idea of being in The Lane alone, but the rest of his friends had gone on earlier. That's what the locals called it, simply "The Lane." He couldn't remember any of them ever saying they had been down The Lane by themselves.

The Lane itself was beautiful, with thick, overhanging trees from each side touching each other and overlapping in the middle, creating shadows for coolness on hot, muggy summer days. You could hear the wind start through the trees down the way, and anticipate the refreshing breeze before it reached you, bringing a much-needed coolness across the face and ruffling hair.

But The Lane had one major problem.

The old Spenser House.

And Colton was almost there. It was just around the curve. Overgrown brush prevented anyone from seeing it before the curve. However, once around the bend, there was the old Spenser House on the right. It may have appeared attractive at one time. But now it was an old board house, dingy white and weather-beaten, window panes missing and the gaps boarded up, roof falling down in spots, weeds overgrown around it.

Although the window panes were missing, the front door was still intact, not boarded up, firmly and completely in place, inviting everyone to keep out. As indeed they did.

Even the toughest teen-age braggarts never tried to go in, not even in daylight.

Of course, there was another way to get to Number Six, and that was by the county road, but that meant going around by way of the sawmill and down the road a ways. And, being late today, it just didn't seem to Colton to be worth the extra time.

There was just something about the place—something that caused the few groups, twosomes or threesomes that sometimes traveled The Lane on foot, to quicken their pace and talk louder as they passed by the old Spenser House.

Dogs passed over to the left side and kept their humans between them and the house, tails tucked between their legs. Or so it was said.

Colton's dog wasn't with him today, but he bet he would not have tucked *his* tail in. He had the most fearless dog in town. Today Colton had called and called and whistled for him, but he hadn't come. Must be across town, Colton had thought. So he had decided to go without him.

Now, as Colton walked around the bend, he started feeling particularly "funny" as he neared the end of the curve. Something *felt* different, but nothing looked different.

Suddenly, as he grew even with the house, the hairs on the back of his neck stood up, causing him to grasp for breath.

"Run! Run!" something said to him. Whether it was something inside or outside his head, he couldn't tell. He didn't take the time to question it.

"Run for your life," the voice, or…whatever …repeated.

Without hesitating, Colton began running. He ran the fastest he had ever run, knowing without a doubt that his life was in danger. From what, or from where, or from whom the danger might come, he didn't know. He only knew he had to get away or face an uncertain but horrible fate. With heart and legs racing, Colton ran until he simply had to slow down. Then, not looking back, but jogging on, he continued down The Lane.

Spotting the last turn before the swimming hole, he stopped, surprised to find he still had his pole and tackle box. Putting them down, he bent double, elbows on knees, breathing heavy, heart pounding.

What was that? he wondered. *Something was there, coming from the Spenser House! But what? I saw nothing! I felt as though I was going to die. But what was it?*

His breathing slowed. He could hear laughter and splashing from the direction of the swimming hole.

Good. He needed others right now. Of course, he couldn't tell anyone how the old Spenser House had spooked him. He'd be the laughingstock all over town by tomorrow. And with the big baseball game being played in a few days, he certainly didn't need that.

He walked slowly around and around in an oval pattern. He knew not to suddenly stop. He had been running too hard.

Having regained his breath back, but still shaking from his ordeal, he headed toward the sounds from the swimming hole. He greeted the swimmers and walked upstream a short way from them to fish. He just didn't have the strength to swim right then.

By the time his stringer was full of perch and he had joined the others to cool off, he was over whatever had happened.

Almost.

But they went home the other way…

எஐஏ

Colton shook his head, drawing his thoughts back to the present.

But what could a house have to do with a disappearance? Unless—could someone be staying there? Could someone have been hiding there for years? Someone no one knew? Perhaps some psycho? After all, no one ever stopped really to check out the place. Its appearance had been enough to scare off any of the kids.

Colton decided to find out all he could about the old Spenser House. He had taken several weeks' vacation, had more coming, if needed. Too many children had disappeared from this sleepy little country town. He was determined to find out why. There had to be a reasonable and plausible explanation. He would use all his resources as a detective to find some answers—and to find Abigail.

What if it was a "sicko" causing the disappearances—someone's likeable, smiling neighbor who no one would suspect in a million years? Was it the past president of the PTA, or someone equally unsuspected?

He would find out. He would start asking enough questions that someone would be nervous and make a mistake. Colton would be watching, listening, and waiting, and he would "nail the sucker."

Not only did his police instincts fire up but also now Colton had a personal interest in finding the kidnapper.

This was early morning. Maybe, just maybe, Abigail would still be alive somewhere if he hurried.

He quickly told Marsha what he planned on doing and that he would see her again as soon as he could. He kissed her long and hard and told her how much he loved her, that he would never let her go again.

Chapter 7

Granny Spenser

A hedgerow completely surrounded Marsha's house. Many of the homes all over town had similar hedges. People had planted the shrubs years ago, let them grow, and kept them trimmed.

It was a poor man's fence, but very effective.

It made a good privacy fence. It was hard to see through it, for the leaves and branches, and impossible for an adult to pass through. As children, they had known all the gaps in the fences around town. They knew where to crawl through as shortcuts going somewhere.

He passed through the Miller's gate and started walking to his car down the block. There was a petite old lady standing on the sidewalk. He had to pass by her to get to his car. He glanced at her, ready to say "Good morning," when something in her eyes made him falter, his steps slow.

Her eyes were clear, steady, looking at him as if piercing his very soul. He had the feeling that, somehow, she knew all about him, yet he had never seen her in his life.

Although it was the middle of summer, she was dressed in a long black dress with a cream-colored, crocheted shawl around her shoulders. Her white hair was pulled back in a bun at the back of her neck, with a small black hat with a red flower on top, on her head.

Her face was old, just how old, Colton could not say.

As he hesitated, she said, "You're the only one who can stop it."

She said it very clearly and plainly while looking straight at him. Colton had no doubt that she was speaking to him.

He knew that voice! Where had he heard her before? He couldn't recall ever having seen her before, yet he had heard the voice.

How frustrating it was to have something just below the surface, refusing to come clear!

Where had he heard her?

He knew it would nag at him, probably causing him to jerk awake in the middle of the night sometime, deciding it was from some movie or another.

But, still…

Her words made no sense, so he thought she was probably senile, saying something to whoever would listen.

"Excuse me," he said. He moved to go around her.

As he did, she repeated, "You're the only one who can stop it."

Colton kept walking. In a fleeting decision, he felt it would be more respectful to the old lady to continue on his way than to stop. Chances were, she wouldn't even remember what she said from one moment to the next.

A few long strides took him to his car and there he turned back to look at her, out of curiosity, if nothing else.

She was gone!

"How could she have moved so fast?" Colton wondered.

There was no place for her to have gone. She had been in the middle of the block with the street on one side and the thick hedgerow on the other.

Colton shook his head.

He didn't have time to worry about crazy old ladies!

Chapter 8

Marsha Remembers

When Colton left, Marsha continued to sit and swing. What she told Colton had been true. She simply could not bear to listen to all the company speculating on where her little girl could be, and what could have happened to her.

Most of the people were in the back of the house, so maybe she could go undetected.

So many happy hours they had spent on this same swing. Only, this time, he had not turned and waved as she had done twelve years ago. Then, he had smiled and waved, so happy to be going away to college. He had promised to write as soon as possible, and, to his credit, he did, within the first week. He told her everything in those letters—dorm life, classes, clubs he wanted to join. He thought she had only planned to go to California for a visit, and then back to Midland, perhaps to work in Fort Smith, or go to the junior college there. At least he had expected her to wait on him, to marry him when he finished college.

She had not answered his letters. She had decided not to, even before she left here. They were forwarded to her in California, her mother made sure of that.

Finally, she had written him, in a separate envelope to her mother, for her to mail from Midland. She had told him, nicely, but firmly, that she had decided to stay in California, that their relationship was over, and that she was dating other men.

She had broken his heart, she knew, with her lies, because the letters kept coming, begging her to reconsider. Eventually, they stopped, as she knew they would. The last one had sworn undying love, which she hoped would change, but now she was glad it had not.

Because she had never stopped loving him.

She rocked gently.

She had not told Colton all she had heard people saying, especially the local sheriff's deputy. On the phone, he had kindled her anger anew at what he had implied. He had spoken in generalities, not knowing Abigail personally. Technically, Abigail was not yet even a missing person. She had only not shown up at bedtime last night and it was not yet noon now. But Abigail was a good girl and not street wise beyond her years. Although she had lived in Southern California until she was almost ten, Marsha had managed to protect her from some of the things other girls that age were already experiencing.

A deputy had come out last night to talk with Marsha because she had been so persistent.

It was those things that the deputy had implied might have taken place. First, he had started asking about boyfriends.

"Boyfriends?" Marsha had echoed, incredulously. "She's only twelve, Officer!"

He had shrugged. "Lots of young ladies already have steady boyfriends by that time, so I thought if she did, she might be with him, might have spent the night with him."

Marsha had been so shocked that she had not responded for several long seconds, just stared at the young man. When she had found her voice, she was beginning to be defensive, insulted that he would even suggest such a thing. "She's not a 'young lady' yet, Officer, she's only a little girl, a twelve-year-old girl," she had said, her anger almost uncontrolled.

"Yes, ma'am, I understand that, but please understand that I have to ask certain questions."

"Of course," Marsha had replied, still not mollified. What kind of mother did he think she was, letting a twelve-year-old go steady?

"Did you or your daughter have any kind of argument yesterday, get angry with each other, yell, say things you regretted, that sort of thing?" he had asked.

"No, no, of course not," she replied, growing more apprehensive. "Why do you ask such a thing? My daughter's missing, and you're just standing here, asking these silly questions!"

Tears had formed in her eyes, threatening to fall.

But the deputy was apparently used to dealing with hysterical mothers, so he remained calm and his voice was steady.

"Yes, ma'am," he said, "but you see, there are lots of runaways on the streets in big cities, that ran away from home when they were eleven, or twelve years old. And whether they lived to regret it or not, most immediately get preyed upon by pimps and others who just sit and watch who gets off the buses. They've learned to spot the young girls right 'off the farm,' so to speak. They start by buying them a meal, pretending to be friends with the young ladies, girls, if you will, then quickly force them into prostitution. And, sometimes, these girls leave home with just a simple argument."

"You're kidding," said Marsha, stunned, "that young?"

"'Fraid so, ma'am."

Had she, herself, led such a sheltered life that she didn't know what was happening in the world? Maybe she just refused to think about it most of the time.

"No," she repeated, "no argument yesterday and usually not at all. Abigail's a good girl, good-natured, too. And she minds me well. No, no arguments."

"Yes, ma'am," the officer repeated, politely.

His voice held just the right tone that Marsha couldn't tell whether he believed her or not. "What you're saying is—you don't really believe my daughter *is* missing, right?"

"Well, ma'am—" he began.

Marsha was slowly getting tired of this man calling her "ma'am."

"We can declare your daughter missing, of course," he continued. "But what about her father. Could he have taken her?"

"There is no father," Marsha had answered.

"Yes, ma'am, but even divorced fathers, without custody, take their children when they have the chance. Sometimes, they are never located."

"There is no father. I mean, of course, there's a father, but we've never been married—"

"Oh," the officer had said, causing Marsha to stop talking.

The way he said "Oh" said a lot. Now, what would he think?

"So, what this means is that you're not going to do anything, look for her or anything, right?"

"Well…" He hesitated. "We'll issue a bulletin, of course…I'm so sorry."

She didn't think he looked or sounded very sorry at

all. "Some maniac or psycho has my little girl out there, doing no telling what to her or with her, and you're standing there, telling me you probably won't do a thing about it. What're the police for, anyway? To protect and serve, or wait and pick up the body?"

Marsha's voice had continued to rise as she grew more and more angry at this man.

"Please, ma'am, calm down—" he began, but Marsha had cut him off.

"Don't tell me to calm down. It's my daughter out there somewhere—" She didn't have a chance to continue because her mother had heard the raised voices and had come out of the house. She put her arms around Marsha's shoulders, turned her around, and led her back into the house.

Marsha had broken down then, crying as she had never cried before, not even when Colton had walked away, on his way to college, out of her life, that August so long ago.

Now she sat, calmly thinking of Colton, knowing he would do anything he could to find Abigail. She smiled to herself, realizing she still had such an idolized view of him. In high school, she thought he could do no wrong. But she had faced the fact that if Colton found nothing, and it was a strong possibility, then she had no choice but to wait 'til the sheriff's department went through its usual routine for missing children. By then Abigail might be dead. Marsha knew in her heart that it would be too late by then. The sheriff would not find her daughter alive.

She squeezed her eyes shut, hoping to prevent the tears from falling.

She was unsuccessful.

Chapter 9

Old Man Ogden Tells His Story

The best source of information was Old Man Ogden. The man had lived in town for as long as anyone could remember. If anyone knew what was happening, he would. Colton felt the old man had not told all he knew.

"Back again, huh, young Mitchell?"

"Mr. Ogden, you've just *got* to help me," Colton began quickly.

The old man sensed the urgency in his voice. "Now, what can a crazy old man like me possibly be able to help you with, young man?"

Ogden was prepared to remain aloof and skeptical

until he felt sure that Colton was ready to listen.

"You're not crazy, and we both know it," Colton said.

"Now, that's not what people around these parts say. Call me crazy for talking all the time, I know. Don't think I don't know what they say about me. I know. Don't care, though."

"Mr. Ogden, you said something earlier that stayed on my mind. You know more about what's going on around here than anyone else. You know *something's* going on and that seems to be more than most people want to admit."

"Well, young Mitchell, what can I do you for?" Ogden asked, looking Colton straight in the eye.

What Colton saw startled him, although he wondered why it should have. What he saw in Mr. Ogden's clear, bright eyes looking right at him, perhaps right through him, was intelligence, understanding, and acknowledgment. Colton understood that Old Man Ogden was accepting him on the same level and, somehow, Colton knew that was an honor. This man was not crazy or even senile, as many people might have thought. Misunderstood was the best word Colton came up with at the moment. And he was right. Old Man Ogden knew something!

"You mentioned earlier the names of several children who have disappeared here in Midland through the years. Little Annie and Kelly I do remember but not the others.

Please, would you tell me what you know about them, especially the dates they disappeared."

"Well, now, let me think," he began, starting to roll a cigarette. "Little Annie you know about. She disappeared summer of 'fifty-seven. How old were you then, Mitchell?"

"Eleven, sir."

"Eleven," Ogden repeated. "Eleven. What a wonderful age to be. Guess you used to swim at Number Six, then?"

"Sure," Colton replied. "We all did. Even the grown-ups."

He answered the old man in a tone that said, yes, but what does swimming at Number Six have to do with this? Let's get on with it.

"Patience, young Mitchell, patience," Ogden said softly.

Colton turned red, wondering if the old man could read minds.

"Next came Lucy, summer of 'sixty. A little older than Little Annie, but not much, I don't think."

"Can you be more specific, Mr. Ogden," Colton asked. "You see, I plan to go down to *The Weekly* and read up on each case and I need to know exact dates. Do you, by any chance, remember the exact dates?"

"Little Annie was June 26, 1957, and Lucy was June 30, 1960. You were still around in 1963 when Kelly disappeared, weren't you?"

"Oh, yeah, I'd forgotten about her. Yes, I graduated in 1964."

"Sure, sure, I remember," Mr. Ogden said. He grinned, showing gaps where teeth were missing. "Did you find your 'fame and fortune?"

How does he know that? Colton wondered, thinking of one of the sentences he had put on his senior prediction, that he was leaving Midland to seek his fame and fortune.

"Just because some of us choose to stay in Midland, don't mean we don't understand, Mitchell. I knew long ago it was meant for me to stay here, and stay 'til you came back."

"What do you mean?" Colton asked. His mind shifted back to the old woman on the sidewalk. "You're not the first person to say something strange like that to me today."

"Eh?" Old Man Ogden asked. "Who else? What did someone say to you?"

"Well, as I went back to my car at the Millers, you know, they live on Oak Street—"

Mr. Ogden nodded. He knew where everyone lived in this town.

"I had to park halfway down the block, because there were several cars along the street in front of their house. When I got to the sidewalk, there was an old woman standing there." Colton told Ogden what the old woman had said and how she was gone when he turned around, almost immediately.

"Hat?" asked Old Man Ogden, "with a red flower on it?"

"Yes," Colton breathed. "You know her?"

"Yes and no," was the old man's enigmatic answer.

"But—"

"Don't rightly know her at all, leastways not anymore. She's just stopped by the store here every so often through the years asking me if he was here yet."

"He?" asked Colton.

"You," Ogden said.

"Me?" Colton asked. He felt he was on the verge of becoming thoroughly confused about this whole thing. It was as if he were caught up in a Keystone Cop movie.

"Yep, you're the one, all right. Why else would you have come back, asking all these questions? Starting to suspect something, are you?" Ogden nodded, as if privy to some secret information.

"I'm not sure what I think I suspect," Colton said with a wave of his hand. "You mentioned other children. That must have been after I left for college."

"Yep. The next 'disappearance' was Tommy, on July 7, 1966.

Colton caught the way the old man said *disappearance*. "You don't think they were simply kidnapped, disappearing that way?" he asked.

Old Man Ogden tapped his cigarette on the side of

the astray before continuing. "Weren't kidnapped at all," he said, a note of finality in his voice.

Well, at least he's *convinced about it,* thought Colton. *Maybe he's known more over the years than he's told.*

"No one would have believed me," Ogden said.

Again, Colton was startled that the old man seemed to know what he was thinking, as if he really could read his mind or hear his thoughts.

"I didn't have anything to do with them, neither," said the old man.

Colton was taken aback.

"I never thought you did," he said.

"I know, I know," Ogden said, "but if I had started talking about them through the years, confirming the things all the disappearances have in common, it would've started some people thinking too much. And you know how dangerous that can be!"

Colton had to smile, in spite of the gravity of the situation. He was right to have come back here. This old man knew and understood more than most people thought.

"Sally was on June 25, 1969, Bob on July 10, 1972, and Junie on June 26, 1975. Young Abigail is ahead of time."

"What do you mean 'ahead of time?'" Colton asked.

"You've been writing these dates down, take a look at them. Starting with Little Annie, a child has disappeared every three years, near the same day, also. But now Abigail disappeared after only two years. That means things are speeding up, and it's time to do something about it."

Old Man Ogden once again looked straight at him, his gaze never wavering.

"Time for *you* to do something about it, young Mitchell."

"I don't understand," Colton said. "You keep saying me. Why me?"

"Don't know. You're just the one, that's all. That's for sure."

He began to nod, his head bobbing up and down on his bony neck. He reminded Colton of those little carnival gadgets people put in the back window of their cars, the bobble-heads, where the heads wiggled up and down as the car stopped or hit bumps.

"But—"

"Stop!" Ogden said, holding up a gnarled hand. "Go read the articles about each disappearance like you said, so you'll have a better understanding, then come back here. *The Weekly* closed up years ago, though."

"I noticed that," Colton responded.

"Yep, too many people and businesses moved away, even the school closed up. The kids went over to Hartford to school. Just weren't enough to keep the school going. Gossip columns didn't even work, 'cause everyone already knew everyone else's business, anyhow!" He chuckled. "The building's still there, though. Everything's been left like the day it closed. Simmons will have the key. Remember where he lives?"

"You mean Charlie Simmons? Is he still living?" Colton asked.

"Yep, he's still living, but his son, Basil, took over back in 'sixty-nine. Tried to keep it going a few years but finally shut the doors. Only places supporting it the last couple of years were the general store and Bob's Nursery. And why should they run ads? No people gonna shop here. Anyway, you'd better get going, time's a wasting."

"Yes, of course."

Colton turned and walked swiftly out of the store, feeling as if Ogden had scolded him for staying too long.

But then he was surprised that he even felt the need to "mind" the old man.

Chapter 10

The Dogs

As he drove across town Colton thought about the dog he had as a boy. *Now, what made me think of that?* he wondered.

He thought about King, his dog. He remembered getting him on his ninth birthday. Some would have called him a stray or a mongrel, but he was the prettiest, friendliest dog in the world to Colton. He was a puppy, only seven weeks old, and all wagging tail, slobbering tongue, and big feet. King would grow into those feet.

When he reached his full growth, he was as big as a German Shepherd. Indeed, he was probably half German Shepherd, with much of the same coloring. What the other half was, no one was sure. But Colton would not have traded him for any other dog in the world.

Colton gave him his name, King, from the white tuft of hair on his otherwise black head. Three inches of white hair made him look so regal. The tip of his tail was white for about three inches and always in motion.

King would not have hurt any of Colton's friends. No matter where King was in the yard, he made a mad dash for the gate wagging his tail by the time one or more of the gang got there. They even tried being quiet and sneaking up to the yard, but it never worked.

King made friends with some of the dogs the other boys owned, but some he never did. Some of the other dogs were just acquaintances and he never tolerated them in the yard, but they kept their distance from King. If they tried to come in the yard, they were met with fierce barks, growls, and bared teeth.

And since King was one of the biggest dogs in town, his territory was undisputed.

The gang talked about how brave and fearless King was, how protective of his people and their property. He didn't seem to be afraid of anything.

Which brought Colton's thoughts to a time when King hadn't acted brave at all, although he tried not to show it, so his people would not notice.

And now that he remembered King, Colton also re-membered Spud, Skipper, Rex, and Spot, all at different times, and in different groups. For whenever any number of the gang walked or rode to Number Six, usually two, three, or more of the dogs went along.

Not aware of it at the time, but looking back now, Colton realized there had been a difference in the dogs whenever they went swimming by way of County Line Road as opposed to when they went down Spenser's Lane. And they did go down Spenser's Lane in large groups.

If the dogs were friends with each other, they had their own adventures as everyone went along—chasing rabbits at the side of the road, jumping up to try to catch bees and butterflies. Sometimes they got into the bushes and came out with so many "stick-tights" on them that everyone stopped and picked the little burrs out of their fur. But even that was fun on a summer day with friends.

If the dogs were not friends, they at least tolerated each other, the boys moving as far from each other as possible to keep the dogs at a distance.

That was just one of the things that made a strange situation seem even stranger, now that Colton thought of it.

Funny about the mind, how things that had happened long ago, which seemingly had no importance at the time, could, in a flash, become crystal clear and have important bearing on something later.

Colton felt the actions of the dogs were important, somehow, but the reason eluded him still. Just beyond the conscious part of his mind, he felt there was something he should be grasping, understanding, yet he failed to make an important connection.

Several times, he remembered, when he and King were going down The Lane, King would be fine until they reached the bend right before the old Spenser House.

Starting off, King would be on the right side of Colton, or darting all over the road, but usually returning to the right side, which was his normal position with Colton, whether Colton was walking or riding his bike. Maybe it started out that way because Colton was right-handed and reaching down to pet King came more natural for him that way.

Whatever the reason, by the time they rounded the bend and reached the old house, King was always on his left side, and very close to him. King never made a sound and he was always right at Colton's leg, nearly bumping against him. And Colton never really paid any attention to King being there, or to the fact that his tail was between his legs, and, yes, thought Colton, his tail *was* between his legs. That beautiful, bushy, proud tail with the white tip always held high and blowing in the breeze, was tucked between King's legs as they passed the old Spenser House. *I never realized,* thought Colton, *or* let *myself notice, because I was so concerned with talking fast to King, walking fast myself past the old house. And what about when several of us went together?*

"Think, Colton," he admonished himself. "You're on to something. Think! Yes, that's it!"

Colton was excited. He pictured a time when he, Louis, Mitch, and Billy were going down The Lane. King was along, of course, and so were Spot and Spud, Mitch and Louie's dogs. Spot and King were not particularly friends with each other, and neither of them were impressed that King just felt them to be beneath him. King disdained a dog that didn't learn when to bark and when not to bark. And what dog needed friends who were not brave and fearless like himself? But he tolerated them on trips like this because he understood that their people were friends of his friend, and that was okay.

The dogs had established their "pecking order" and King was at the top. He always jogged in front of the boys. If none of his dog pals were along, he just politely led the way, ignoring the other dogs. Spot and Spud recognized his authority and were content to trot along beside their human friends.

That was the normal order on most of The Lane. But the portion of The Lane in front of the old Spenser House was anything but normal, except in appearance.

And Colton remembered one particular day.

Without realizing it, or thinking about it, by the time the boys turned the bend all the dogs were on the left side of the boys, side by side or close together somehow, as close as the three dogs could get, all three with tails between their legs, and ears back.

Colton recalled this happening anytime more than one dog went with them and he knew, now, without any doubt, it was the only time King, or any of the other dogs, allowed themselves to get that close to each other.

But there was something about the old Spenser House that let them instinctively come together for protection, to put their people between them and the house. Once safely past the house, the order and positions were once again assumed, almost casually, without fanfare, almost as if the dogs were ashamed of having moved to the left together that way, and trying not to let their people know they had done so for that short period of time.

Colton knew, also, that such actions were then never mentioned among the dogs again, just as the same rule kept the boys from talking about certain things.

After all, the dogs had to maintain their honor and pride, also.

As the boys talked louder and walked quicker past the house, they never paid attention to the dogs. Clearly, now, Colton could see every time it had happened. Each time flashed across his mind.

"I should have thought of this a few minutes ago," he chided himself. How did Spud act whenever he and his best friend, Louie, walked down The Lane together? And he knew they had walked that way, although Spud wasn't with him that day Colton saw him. And that was strange in itself.

Just like King and Colton were inseparable, whenever you saw Spud first, you knew Louie would show up in a few seconds, or the other way around.

I'll have to ask him about Spud, Colton thought, *but another time.*

But it was important, he knew it was. It said something and he was going to find out what. If the dogs sensed something, like the boys did, perhaps even the same thing, the same feeling, then something was there. And if it was anything to do with Abigail, Colton was going to find out.

Good old King. Dead for many years now but helping to solve the problem.

"Wait!"

Colton threw on the brakes, bringing his car to a skidding halt in the middle of the street. He looked out the front for as far as he could see, and then twisted around in the seat, his arm across the back, to look at the back.

Then to both sides.

He was on a residential street, with houses on both sides, beautifully kept lawns and shrubs in most cases. Typically, there was the one that had an unkempt yard, an old car with a flat parked out front.

There's always at least one, he thought, shaking his head.

Since it was summer, flowers and shrubs bloomed everywhere. Flowerbeds were bright splashes of color and sidewalks, and side yards were lined and covered with colorful blooms.

The gentle breeze he had felt earlier rustled through

the trees and shrubs that lined the street. But he wasn't concerned with the aesthetics of the area. As far as he could see, there were no dogs. Was that just a coincidence? Maybe he was just on a street that had no outside dogs, maybe just inside pets.

Cats? he wondered. *Any cats around?*

He couldn't see any cats, either. Which still might just have been a coincidence.

But, thinking back, even if not everyone or even the majority of the people on any given street had dogs—cats?—it seemed there was always one crossing from one street to another, lying in a yard or on the sidewalk.

Colton decided to take two or three minutes to drive up and down a few streets to see if he could spot any dogs or cats.

This was a Saturday morning. There should be lots of boys and girls out playing and that meant dogs would be with them.

He slowly turned the corner. He took a route that had many houses on it. The first turn brought him meeting three boys on bicycles, baseball gloves on the handlebars.

Yes, they're headed the right way, he thought. He knew the baseball park was several blocks behind him.

But no dogs ran along beside them.

You can't tell me that not even one of those boys has a dog.

He wanted to look more, but only a minute.

"Abigail is still alive—and you know she is," a voice

told him, "so you can't spend time looking for dogs or cats.

Next, he spotted two girls sitting on the steps of the porch, playing with their dolls.

He didn't see a dog.

A few houses down, three small children were splashing in a rubber swimming pool while a woman sat nearby and watched. The man was watering the flower-bed and squirting the kids every once in a while, which brought delighted squeals from them.

A happy, perfectly normal domestic scene on a summer day.

But no dogs around.

Colton had driven by as slowly as he dared, so as not to arouse suspicion or draw attention to himself. They hadn't even looked his way.

Several more turns onto several more streets and Colton was convinced. He had spotted several children in various acts of play, but no pets.

"That's not right," he said out loud. "That's just not right at all. Something's very wrong with this town."

Chapter 11

Colton Visits the Simmons

He knew where Mr. and Mrs. Simmons lived. Mrs. Simmons used to give the kids milk and cookies on her front porch. He guessed she thought that was something she could do for them, since their house was close to the ball field.

He remembered her crying about Little Annie.

Colton drove to the Simmons' house almost automatically. This sleepy little town had not changed in all the years he had been gone. By change, he knew he subconsciously meant, "grown." Because the town definitely *had* changed.

Once thriving "Mom and Pop" stores had all closed

up. The cafes were boarded up. Most of the buildings were still there, just boarded up or locked tight with a general, long-time, unused look about them.

There certainly wasn't any use in trying to sell the land or the buildings. Who would want them and for what? For the past twenty years, young people of the town had moved away as soon as they graduated from high school. Most never moved back and those who moved to Fort Smith just made the usual weekend trip back home to visit parents or grandparents. If they had moved farther away, the occasional holiday trip seemed to be enough.

When the elementary school closed, the teachers involved moved away. Without an elementary school in town, young parents had no reason to buy a home there. They cited their choices of other towns as wanting to get their children closer to school. In the natural order of things, without the families, there was no commerce, so the stores begin closing one by one.

The only ones left were Adams who owned the general store—and he was old enough and had enough money, anyway, that he didn't have to worry about customers—and the feed store. And the locals did appreciate the fact that these were still in business, if only for the one or two items they usually forgot from the supermarket or Wal-Mart in Fort Smith.

But Colton remembered a thriving country town, complete with traffic lights and trains.

So now, except for one or two missing, the houses were the same. He quickly went to the Simmons' place. Old Man Ogden hadn't definitely said anything about Mr. Simmons, only that his son had taken over the newspaper. Whichever, Colton knew either one would let him into the building to look at back issues of the paper.

He didn't particularly want them to know what he was looking for, or why, so he thought he'd better come up with a reason for wanting to look at the old papers. Mrs. Simmons may have given the boys and girls milk and cookies but he remembered, his mother talking about what a "busybody" she was, how she always needed— and somehow seemed—to be the first to know everyone's business.

His mother had often wondered out loud if maybe Mrs. Simmons didn't write the newspaper articles. If he didn't want everyone still living here to know he was starting to investigate the missing children, then he'd better have another reason.

Research! Of course! He could say he was working on a paper about small towns in America.

Two people were on the front porch of the house, in the swing at the end. Seniors. One of them turned her head as he started up the steps.

Mrs. Simmons smiled, a friendly smile that showed false teeth. Her face was a mass of wrinkles.

"Colton Mitchell," she said.

She started to get up out of the swing.

The old man had not turned his head at his approach.

"No, no, don't get up, Mrs. Simmons," Colton said.

She sank back down, gratefully, Colton thought.

"Haven't seen you in so long, how many years?" she asked and then continued before Colton could say anything. "You and the other boys used to come to this very porch for milk and cookies. I haven't made cookies in so long, I think I've forgotten how. It's good of you to come to see an old woman like this. Are you on vacation? Where are you living now—"

Colton felt her questions were in danger of becoming endless, so he interrupted.

"It's a working vacation, I'm afraid," he began, prepared to present his story of research. "How are you and Mr. Simmons these days?"

He looked questioningly at the figure sitting next to her.

"Mr. Simmons has Alzheimer's, I'm afraid," she said. "But he's as well as can be expected, I suppose. Basil and Martha came to live with us a few years back to take care of us."

She smiled again. "What are you working on a vacation for?"

"I'm doing research for a paper on small-town America. I was hoping I could get the key to *The Weekly* building and go through some of the old newspapers, just for some information."

"Of course you can," she said. "Just knock on the

door there for Basil. Sometimes they're in the back of the house."

Colton knocked several times on the screen door before Basil came, a smile on his face.

"Mitchell," he said, holding out his hand. "How are you?"

Colton shook his hand. "How is it that everyone in this town recognizes me?" he asked. He thought he had changed quite a lot since he had left this place.

"Look just like you did in high school," Basil responded. "How's your dad these days—"

Before he could answer, Mrs. Simmons interrupted.

"Colton needs the key to *The Weekly*," she said. "He wants to see the old newspapers for some research. I told him he could have the key."

"Sure," Basil agreed, "under one condition, and that is that you don't harm a thing—some of those papers are collectors' items by now. I keep telling myself I'm going to bring them all to the house here, but never have. What are you doing research on?"

The lie again. But a necessary one. "I'm writing on the evolution of small towns in America. I haven't decided just yet what direction I'll take with the paper."

Basil nodded his head. "For a second there I thought you might be interested in our resident kidnapper."

Colton caught his breath, looking sharply at Basil. Maybe here was some information he needed to help solve the disappearances. These people around here seemed to throw out things at odd times, totally unaware that what they said might be of interest to someone.

Colton pretended innocence. "Resident kidnapper?"

"How old are you? When did you leave here, anyway?" Basil asked.

"I'm thirty. I left here in 1964."

"Then you're old enough to remember. If you want to remember, that is."

"Remember?" Colton asked.

He was repeating everything again, in the same Keystone Cop movie but with different characters this time.

"Little Annie disappeared, then Lucy. Dad's never been the same since Lucy disappeared."

Colton looked at him questioningly. "She was Bobby's girl. You know, my brother."

"Oh, yeah," Colton responded.

"She was Dad's favorite grandchild. Always wondered if the shock of her disappearance didn't bring on the Alzheimer's quicker." Basil shook his head. "It's like someone comes back every three years and takes a child from our town. Either that, or it's one of our 'good' neighbors, disguised, of course, as good. I wonder if someone's garden isn't full of children's bodies. You remember?"

Colton nodded. He tried not to appear too eager to hear everything he could about this. He wanted Basil to talk, to recall all he knew. Anything he heard could be important.

"Problem is," Basil continued, "these children seem to disappear into thin air, right off the street."

Something caught Colton's attention.

"Did they disappear off the *same* street, by any chance?" he asked. Why that particular thought came to him, he didn't know.

"Well, I—" Basil seemed baffled. "You know, I can't remember if it was or not—"

He looked sharply at Colton. "Do you think that would mean anything?"

Colton just shrugged, appearing to dismiss the subject. He hoped he didn't appear too interested to give himself away.

"Just a thought. They never found the guy, huh?"

"Nope, not a clue, none of the times," Basil replied.

Since Basil hadn't mentioned the recent disappearance of Abigail, Colton wondered if he even knew about it yet. Marsha had said they were trying to keep it quiet, hoping she had just spent the night somewhere, not letting anyone know she was angry with her mother.

Somehow, Colton knew it wasn't as simple as that, especially since he had talked with Old Man Ogden and seen the old woman.

"Thought for the first couple of disappearances it could have been, you know, bums, transients, coming in on the train, having their way with the girls, burying them somewhere, then hopping a train out of town again. But the last two happened after the train stopped coming through these parts. People moved out who had little girls, and no one has moved in, except for a few families who probably haven't heard about the disappearances. I doubt anyone would tell them. And the next one scheduled to disappear isn't due for another year yet. Some of us are already making plans to catch the guy next time."

Colton never understood why people automatically assumed a kidnapper of children had to be a man. There were some women who would do anything, perhaps more, than any man. In his work, he had encountered many mean, very cruel, women.

He knew the "bum" theory wasn't right. He didn't know how he knew and could never have explained it. He just knew. This was bigger, harder to explain than simple kidnapping.

He was glad when Basil went into the house and returned with the key to *The Weekly* building. He couldn't let Basil see how much of a hurry he was in. But he had one more question.

"You said families with little girls moved out, Colton asked. "That's one thing I noticed—little boys playing and riding bicycles, but only a few little girls. Now I know why. And there's something else maybe you can explain."

"What's that?" Basil asked.

"Where are all the dogs and cats? There used to be animals all over the place. You couldn't drive down a street without having to stop to let a dog or cat cross, or even go around one laying the middle of the street that didn't bother to move for a mere car."

"Funny you should ask," Basil said with a shrug. "No one knows. Maybe there's something growing around here that they eat, then crawl off and die. After people replaced their pets enough times, they just quit getting any. Someone talked once about having the water checked to see if it was harmful to animals but not to humans but I'm not sure anyone ever did. Actually, I think people were glad not to have dogs around to keep them awake at night with their barking or cats around to dig in their flowerbeds. At least no one's complained now that they're gone, wishing we had one every few feet!"

Colton didn't ask any more about the animals, when they started disappearing, or anything. Obviously, people had not related the missing animals with the missing children, and he didn't want them to now. After all, maybe they had nothing to do with each other. *But I know they do.*

He startled himself with the thought. Again, he had no idea how he knew, just that he was very certain.

"There's a definite connection and I'm going to find it," he vowed, as he started down the street, after saying good-bye to Mrs. Simmons.

Mr. Simmons still did not know he had been there.

Chapter 12

The Weekly

Colton was amazed when he stepped into the old print shop. From the old hand-carved counter separating the print equipment from the general public to the old hand-operated equipment itself, the place was an antique collector's dream.

"Did they really print the newspaper with this stuff?" he mused. "No wonder they only did it once a week. It would have taken them that long to print everything!"

Hand-set print type was neatly stored against one wall, covered with clear plastic, as was all the equipment.

Colton had never doubted the print quality of *The Weekly*. It had been superb quality. But that they had done it all on this equipment was incredible.

"A lost art, for sure," he said.

But he wasn't here to admire the machinery. Basil had told him where to find the back issues of the newspaper and he needed to get right to work. Basil had assured him there was at least one copy of every issue of *The Weekly*, beginning with the first issue in 1950.

The shelves were neatly labeled by year, so Colton had no trouble finding 1957. He found a stool, pulled it over to the wall, and sat down to go through the pile he removed from the shelf. At this point, he was grateful *The Weekly* had been just that, a weekly publication. A daily would have taken up too much time. Searching through fifty-two issues a year would go quickly.

He was sure the stories about the missing girls would be front-page news in this little town, and he was right.

The front page of the first paper he found, one dated the first week in July, 1957, read:

YOUNG GIRL MISSING!

(Midland). Little Annie Mercer, eleven-year-old daughter of George and Annie Mercer, 115 Maple Street, Midland, was reported missing by her mother when she failed to return home last Friday evening.

Annie had left her home shortly after noon on Friday to go to ball practice. According to other players on the team, Annie never showed up for practice. Although they commented to each other how unusual it was for Annie to miss practice, they simply thought that perhaps some-thing had come up with her parents, so they said nothing to their parents immediately after practice.

When Annie failed to come home by suppertime, Mrs. Mercer started calling around, expecting to find her daughter eating at someone else's house.

But Little Annie always called her mother if she went home with someone else. At this point, she found out that Annie had not been at ball practice.

By Saturday afternoon, members of the South Sebas-tian County Sheriff's Department were organizing search parties to comb the weeds and fields around Midland.

On Sunday, the sheriff's department brought in their best bloodhound, Sniffles, who led the search party down Elm Street to Spenser's Lane.

This trail came to a halt when Sniffles stopped in front of the old Spenser House.

Sniffles lost the scent and trail at that point. The dog seemed confused, circling a spot on the road, then exhib-iting erratic and unusual behavior.

The deputies were bewildered at the dog's behavior. Not only is Sniffles the Department's best bloodhound, but she always "gets her man."

She apparently went around in circles, chasing her tail, then jumped and snapped at the air, barking fiercely. Along with that, the dog would stop periodically, cower down, and whimper, with her tail between her legs.

After taking the dog back to the Mercer house, start-

ing again, for several times, and having the dog display the same unusual behavior, the search party decided to do a complete search of the old Spenser House. A search had not been done the previous day since the house was obviously boarded up and very overgrown.

A search of the place, however, was unrevealing as to the missing girl's whereabouts. Deputies said it was obvious no one had been near the place in years and years. There was no trampled-down grass or broken bushes, like there would be, if someone had walked around the windows or the back of the house. All windows were still nailed tight and boarded shut and no one had tampered with them. The front door would not open under extreme pressure. The parts of the house they could see through cracks in the boarded-up windows revealed nothing.

Following other leads in the case, they checked train schedules and questioned any known "hobos" who had come through the area in the last few days. The sheriff's office had no suspects, however, after questioning several men.

After searching the area around Midland again on Monday for clues, the *deputies gave up the search, but promised to keep on top of the case.*

Little Annie was last seen wearing blue pedal pushers, white blouse, white socks and white sneakers, and a blue and white "Midland" ball cap. She always had a blue barrette in her hair for ball practice. She had a baseball glove, ball, and bat with her, which they found on Elm Street. She has light brown hair, blue eyes, and weighs 125 lbs., a very stocky girl. Is anyone sees a person fitting this description, please contact the South Sebastian County Sheriff's Department.

Colton found the next article, about Lucy Killan. The paper was dated the Wednesday following her disappearance, in 1960.

The headline, in the same type and size as the previous one, three years before, read:

LITTLE GIRL KIDNAPPED!

(Midland). Late Monday evening, Mrs. Seth Killan called the Sebastian County Sheriff's Department to report that her eleven-year-old daughter, Lucy, was missing. Lucy had left her home to go swimming around noon on Monday, riding her bike to Number Six, via County Line Road. She was alone, several of her friends having gone on earlier. Mrs. Killan had kept Lucy home to clean her room before she allowed her to go swimming.

Reports from other children later that evening revealed that Lucy never reached Number Six. Her bicycle, a blue Western Flyer, was found on Elm Street, between Maple and Spenser's Lane, in the afternoon by Billy Watson, who took it to the Killan home. He said he thought Lucy had just forgotten she left it there, so he leaned it against the side of the detached garage, the side away from the house. It was assumed that both Lucy and the bicycle were missing until Billy heard his parents talking about Lucy and told them about the bicycle. They immediately called the Killans.

Before the bicycle was found, the sheriff's department thought that perhaps Lucy had simply changed her mind about swimming and had bicycled to a friend's house instead. She even had relatives in the country where she had bicycled to before, who could not be reached by phone.

But interviews with friends and relatives revealed no information to her whereabouts.

Authorities are now speculating that someone, or several people in a car or van, stopped Lucy on the corner, and then forced her into the vehicle, leaving the bicycle on the street, and kidnapped Lucy Killan.

At this printing, the sheriff's department has decided to bring in a bloodhound to see if they can trace the little girl that way.

Lucy Killan was last seen wearing red shorts, a white blouse, red anklets, and sneakers. Her hair was pulled back in a ponytail, with a rubber band. She had a red/yellow/blue-flowered one-piece bathing suit on under her outer clothes. She was carrying a large red bath towel. Billy said the towel was not on the bicycle when the found the bike. Lucy has blonde hair, brown eyes, and weighs approximately 85 lbs.

If anyone sees a child answering this description, please contact the Sebastian County Sheriff's office.

Chapter 13

Lucy

July 1960:

As Lucy kicked the kickstand on her bicycle, pushed it back and up with her foot, she wished she had cleaned her room yesterday like her mom had told her. As a result, her mom had made her do it this morning, and now she was late going swimming with all her friends. She shoved her red towel into the basket on front of her handlebars.

She gave the bike a shove, swinging up on the seat. She had gotten this bike last Christmas and was very proud of it. She took good care of it and only let a few of her very best friends ride it. She never, ever laid it down on the ground, instead always using the kickstand.

But now she was late. She worried that by the time she got to Number Six, everyone would be tired and finished swimming.

As she approached the corner of Maple and Elm, she thought, *Why not take Spenser's Lane to Number Six?* After all, she *was* late.

Of course, she had heard, like everyone else, that Spenser's Lane was spooky, just downright creepy. No one had really ever said why, though, so she decided to take it. It would only take a few minutes on her bike, and she would pump as fast as she could.

When she turned on Elm, she was still just cruising, saving her energy to go fast down The Lane.

Before she realized it, Lucy felt herself slowing down. It was probably just the undergrowth. She had not realized how overgrown this narrow path really was.

She tried to renew her efforts at pumping her bike, which had always been so easy to pump. She went a few more yards at normal speed, but again felt herself slowing down.

She stopped her bike, leaning over on one foot, the other still on a pedal.

Maybe I'll just walk a bit, get my energy back. It'll pass if I take it easy for a few minutes.

She took the bath towel out of the basket, threw it over her right shoulder, and began pushing her bicycle along. Before she knew it, she had stopped again. She pushed it a few more feet.

Lucy decided to leave her bike and continued walking. She walked as fast as she could through the tall grass and weeds. She thought about going back but since she was almost past the old Spenser House, she decided just to get by it as quickly as she could.

As she came to the front of the house, she started running, remembering what everyone said about the old place.

Just

Just don't

Just don't go

Just don't go down

Just don't go down Spenser's

Just don't go down Spenser's Lane by yourself

EVER

Do

Do you

Do you hear

Do you hear me?

The words of the chant they used as they jumped rope brought to mind everything else she had ever heard.

I shouldn't be here. Why am I here? I have to go back!

Before she could react, she heard a rustling in the tall grass beside her. As she turned to see what was making the sound, her eyes opened wide.

She opened her mouth to scream just as it was clamped shut. Her struggles to break free were futile as another arm quickly enveloped her.

She tried to struggle and free herself, but the grip was too tight. She was not aware that one of her tennis shoes came off.

Lucy was carried toward the open door of the house. Her towel fell off her shoulder, landing on a bramble bush.

Her other tennis shoe fell off, first one and then another as she gave a few feeble kicks in the air.

Her feeble kicks were stopped by a simple snap of her neck.

Lucy didn't know her shoes had come off.

Lucy didn't know anything again…ever.

Chapter 14

Otis

Otis Ledbetter saw the little girl standing in The Lane. He smiled and raised his hand to wave to her, just as he had waved to her many times as she rode by his house on her bicycle. She always smiled at him, waving, saying something that was lost in the wind, which Otis took as a greeting.

But Otis lowered his hand when he realized the girl hadn't even seen him.

She turned to face the old house.

His mama had told him about the old house, so he had never gone across the road to it. He was afraid of it. In fact, he hardly ever came across the field this way to

The Lane, only every once in a while. He knew boys and girls came this way sometimes, going somewhere.

Once he had decided to follow them to see where they went. He found them in a creek, splashing around, pushing and pulling each other, sometimes going under the water and not coming up for a while.

Otis had stayed out of sight. His mama had warned him about going into water like that, so he thought it would hurt him. He thought it was hurting the boys and girls, and it upset him.

He had turned around and run home, rocking on the front porch for the rest of the day. He wouldn't tell his mama what was wrong.

So, Otis didn't come this way very often. Only sometimes, he came to check to see if anyone had dropped anything that he could pick up and add to his treasure in the sheds. His mama let him keep the pretty things he found. Once he found a good towel that she washed and they started using.

Right now, though, while he was wondering in his limited way what was wrong with the little girl, something reached out from the bushes beside her and pulled her out of his sight. She gave a few little kicks, which caused one of her tennis shoes to come off. He watched with his heart pounding as the little girl was carried toward the old house. Close to the house her other shoe fell off.

He had never seen anyone do that before, but he

knew he didn't know what others knew, so maybe this was okay.

But, for some reason, it upset him seeing the little girl carried into the old house like that. It didn't seem quite right but he didn't know why. Sure, his mama had always told him that he wasn't like other people, so maybe this was okay.

He decided to take her shoe, the first one that had come off, the one nearest to him. If nothing else, she would try to find it later—he was always trying to find his shoes—and she would smile and wave at him again.

He hesitated before stepping across the ditch to pick up her shoe. What if she was looking out from the old house and saw him? She'd think he was stealing it. His mama had taught him the difference between stealing something and just finding something.

Finally, he jumped the ditch, grabbed the shoe, turned, jumped the ditch again, and ran home across the field.

His mother heard the rocker and came out of the house. She could not get him to tell her what upset him this time. As long as he was here, rocking, he was okay, so she didn't worry. A lot of things, sometimes very simple things to other people, upset him, so she went about her business of canning.

She'd just heard him open and shut the door to one of the sheds so he probably had seen a mouse or a snake. They always scared him.

Come to think of it, though, she hadn't seen a lot of mice around lately, not since the cat had disappeared.

Oh, well. He was home. That was the important thing.

By tomorrow, he would have forgotten whatever upset him today.

Chapter 15

Bloodhound Loses Trail

July 1976

Colton looked at the paper for the following Wednesday. He wanted to know what happened with the bloodhound.

He had thought about going into Fort Smith and looking up everything in the Fort Smith paper, the *Southwest Times Record*, but since it would take at least an hour just to get there, and they might not even be open on Saturday, he had decided that whatever he found in *The Weekly* would have to be enough. Besides, being local, he figured it just might contain more facts and personal information than a larger, more distant paper.

He was right. A larger newspaper probably would not have included Billy, just the fact that the bike was found.

Colton particularly wanted to know how the dog acted, where the scent took it.

Here it was a front-page article again.

BLOODHOUND LOSES TRAIL

(Midland). On Tuesday, the Sebastian County Sheriff's office brought in Trudy, their number one bloodhound, in the search for Lucy Killan, an eleven-year-old girl missing since Friday. Trudy has been used in several successful searches and only six months ago replaced Sniffles, an older dog, as lead dog for the Department.

Trudy picked up the scent on the corner of Maple and Elm Streets, using Lucy's bicycle as a starter.

She immediately started leading the searchers to and down Spenser's Lane. Without hesitation, the dog went trotting off down Spenser's Lane. Then the dog apparently lost the scent in front of the old Spenser House. She stopped abruptly, circling a spot for several minutes, trying to pick up where the trail went from there.

Unable to pick up a trail, the dog, at one time, sat down on her haunches, put her nose in the air, and howled. This startled the deputies, who said she had never acted that way before.

Several minutes of circling followed, with periods of jumping and snapping at the air, followed then by howling. The dog seemed very confused and frustrated, then alternately whimpering and hiding behind the men with its tail between its legs.

The officers repeatedly said they'd never seen anything like it. However, one of the officers on the scene, who had worked on the force for years and with the canines, said he had seen this once before—when Sniffles had been brought in to try to locate "that other little girl some years back."

The officer was referring to the case of Little Annie Mercer, who disappeared approximately three years ago from approximately the same spot, at least according to Sniffles, the dog on the case at the time. According to the officer, Sniffles had led the search party then to this same spot but no clues were discovered in that case.

As then, no other clues were uncovered now in the search of Lucy Killan. As before, Trudy was taken back to the beginning of the trail—Maple and Elm Streets—three times, and she returned to the same spot, each time displaying the same behavior as before.

The sheriff's department admitted to being baffled by the case and they said they would continue to investigate every clue in hopes of finding the little girl and solving the case.

Chapter 16

Granny Spenser Returns

Colton cursed himself for not having a notepad with him. Maybe he had thought this place would have a copier, like all modern newspapers and libraries, and he would have had a copy of the articles in a few minutes.

"Just shows you how spoiled we've become to these things," he said to himself. Talking out loud seemed to help dispel the quietness and gloominess of the place.

He remembered his billfold-sized Franklin Quest planner and knew he had some extra pages in that. He stood up to remove his billfold from his back pocket. He glanced toward the front window. His hand stopped halfway to his hip.

There in the plate-glass window, standing on the out-side looking in at him, was the little old lady he had en-countered on Marsha's street. She could see him clearly, as he had opened the blinds for better light upon entering the building.

When she saw him looking at her, she began nodding her head, as if in approval of his actions.

This is incredible, Colton thought, starting to the front of the room. *She must know something.*

Since he had to walk the length of the front counter and then go back around it to the front door, it took sev-eral seconds. Colton felt like it was taking him forever to reach the door. Throwing it open wide, he stepped quick-ly onto the sidewalk, knowing that it had actually taken him only a few seconds to reach the front. This time, he would face her and ask questions.

To his surprise and consternation, the old lady was nowhere to be seen. As the window she had looked in was in the middle of the building, he wondered how she could have moved so quickly, probably going around to the side, since she was not on the sidewalk in either direc-tion.

Only one side would have allowed her to go around the building, so he went that way, rounding the corner as quickly as possible. She was not at the side, so he contin-ued around to the back.

Nothing. No one. She was not there. Neither was she going across the open yard at the back and side of the building. He moved to check the other side, although he knew she could not be here. This side and back were fenced in with a fairly new barbed-wire fence, by the look of it.

Still no one.

"I know she didn't just vanish into thin air," he said. *Or did she?*

He was shocked that the thought had come to him, but she had no place to go to in the middle of the block, either, and not enough time to go anywhere—yet, she was certainly not here.

"Or maybe she was never here to begin with," he said. "Colton, old boy, and you're just getting spooked and imagining things with this whole business."

That had to be it. And here he had lost valuable reading time looking for a little old lady who didn't exist.

Yet, deep down, he knew he had actually seen someone both times. The first time this person told him, in a voice he knew—yet couldn't place—that he was the only one that could stop it—whatever "it" was. And, now, the same person had nodded her head, in approval, it seemed, at what he was doing.

And what was he doing? Finding out all he could about the missing girls, in hopes of finding Abigail alive, that was what he was doing.

But how would the old lady even *know* that was what he was doing? The only one he had talked to before he saw the old lady the first time had been Old Man Ogden and Colton had gone straight from there to Marsha's. There was no way anyone could have beaten him to that street.

And, now, he had come straight to the newspaper building from the Simmons'. Of course, she did show up later each time, as if she happened to overhear the conversation with Ogden then later at the Simmons' house. That was the only way Colton could figure that she would know where he was headed. But why should a little old lady care what he was doing?

Stranger and stranger, he thought, as he settled back on the stool to copy all he could about Little Annie. At least he would get a description of what she looked like and what she was wearing the day she disappeared, if nothing else.

He made notes then neatly put the newspapers back in the stack and the stack neatly back in place on the shelf.

Basil was right. Colton knew the man had a gold mine with these old papers.

Probably knows what he's got in this old equipment, too. He's just waiting for the right time to get rid of it.

☙❧

Colton felt it coming, just as he had felt every one before.

It started with a feeling on the back of the neck, the

sort of feeling that made you want to reach up and swipe away a gnat or mosquito or something else that may have landed there.

After that feeling, his vision started closing in, beginning with little black spots that appeared at the edge of his eyes, then the black grew bigger and bigger until it covered the whole eye.

The "picture" appeared. Colton called them "pictures," for lack of a better term. He was awake, he knew he was awake—there was no question of that. It was always in the middle of something he was doing, and he had to stop momentarily, just for a second, because this took over, whatever it was.

In the pictures, he always saw a little girl. She was dressed in shorts and a blouse, had "dishwater" blonde hair, something on her head, and it seemed as if Colton should know her. But he couldn't place her, couldn't see who it was, because of one thing.

The girl was faceless.

There was just a blob, a shadow where her face should be. And that was the worst thing of all. The girl was talking to him, and he knew it was important, something he should know. But his mind would will the vision away, every time.

But—wait—

The image of the other person was coming to him. It was a boy, about the same age as the girl, and this was the person the girl was talking to.

Colton was excited, yet scared. The feeling was always scary. This was more than he usually saw. And now he understood something. Not only was his mind trying to wave the image away but the boy in the picture was waving the girl away with an impatient gesture.

That fit. Boys of that age always were impatient with girls, not wanting them tagging along and all.

And now. The boy was turning away from the girl, toward Colton, as if toward a movie camera, Colton being the camera.

No! No—how—why?"

It was himself as a boy. The face was clearly one he had seen in many photos he had of his childhood. There was no doubt about it. It was him. But who was the girl? What did it mean?

Colton looked at the girl again, but her face was still not there. She turned away slowly, sadly it seemed, a girl rejected by the boy she admired, her affection refused.

The picture started fading, as it always did. Light began returning to Colton' eyes, slowly, from the center out. Gradually he could see where he was, in the old print shop.

He slumped, hanging his head, knowing there was something in these images that he needed to know, and yet not being able to grasp the meaning. These had started a little over a year ago, just about the time he started thinking it would be nice to visit the old hometown again, see how it had changed, who might still be around.

If only he knew what the little girl was saying to him or who she was. By the clothes and hair he had no recognition of anyone he could remember. The clothes and hair could have belonged to millions of little girls back then.

At least he knew it was "back then," because he himself had appeared this time, perhaps at eleven or twelve years of age. The girl was about the same age.

Colton could only sit a minute. He felt so drained, just as he had after each of these visions. Yet they only lasted a few seconds.

Several times, it had happened with others around him yet no one ever noticed anything different about him. He did not have seizures, faint away, scream, or react in any physical way, except for the extreme bout of tiredness that followed. Everything occurred in split second time within his own psyche.

And now he had witnessed more than he ever had. Was it because he was now in Midland and this image was from his childhood here? Was he getting closer to what it meant?

The only thing he could think of from his childhood, which could cause any mental anguish, *was* the missing girls, and he had forgotten about them through the years.

Or had he?

Now that he was working on it, was something about to be revealed to him?

He knew it was no good trying to conjure up the images on his own. He had tried that before. They just seemed to come and go whenever they wanted. Nothing before had seemed to make a connection, but now he knew that, somehow, it had something to do with his being here.

He had begun to doubt the sanity and rationality of what he was doing, that being trying to find Abigail and. perhaps in the process, finding out what happened to the other girls who had disappeared. After all, if no one before him had been able to solve the case, why did he think he could do it?

Just as he was doubting himself, the picture had returned, revealing more than ever before.

There is *something here,* he thought. *Something taking the lives of children on a consistent basis, yet years apart. Psychos simply don't wait that long, and sex fiends certainly don't.*

"What, what, what is it?" he cried, putting his head in his hands. "Think!"

It had to be in the reports. There were obvious connections, things that were the same. He needed to read the articles all again, taking notes of what things were the same, and then what was different in each case.

In a way, he thought he might be wasting his time, yet he had to start somewhere. Colton had laid all the newspapers he needed along the old counter, when he heard a knock on the door.

Who? he wondered, thinking of the old lady.

It was Marsha.

"What are you doing here?" he asked, sounding more abrupt than he intended to, yet he was glad to see her. Maybe he needed company in this old building, where the ghosts of former workers seemed to linger in the shadows, guarding the results of all the years of sweat and tears they put into the articles, now spread before these two.

"I couldn't just keep sitting, listening to all those people, and wondering what might have happened to Abigail. I thought maybe I could help you," she replied, in a pleading tone, hoping he wouldn't tell her to leave.

"Sure, you can," Colton said. "Come on, I'll show you what I've found and what I'm doing."

He showed her the articles, pointing out all the dates.

"The answer is here somewhere. And here's an interesting article I ran across," he told her, holding up the paper on the end of the row. "It has nothing to do with the disappearances, at least I don't think it does. But it caught my eye."

Marsha took the newspaper, holding it up in such a position to get the best lighting on it. She read the same articles he had read.

"You're right. It's very interesting. But I don't remember any stories, do you?"

"No," Colton agreed, "and I have no idea why it caught my attention. It just seemed to jump out at me. Oh, well." He shrugged, laying the newspaper back down, dismissing it.

"Let's get to work,"

"What are we looking for, specifically?" Marsha asked.

"I'm not sure," he replied. "Just all the facts that are similar, first, then we'll look at the differences. But we need to do it as quickly as possible. Every second counts. I *know* Abigail's alive but we have to hurry."

When he mentioned Abigail's name, Marsha looked up with tears in her eyes.

Colton took her hand, pulling her to him.

"Don't cry. Please," he whispered into her hair. "We'll find her."

"Do you really think so?" she asked, pushing slightly away from him, looking up into his face.

"Yes, I do," he answered, firmly and was rewarded with a small smile.

What did she expect him to say?

"Sorry," she said. "Let's get to work."

For the next few minutes, they read quickly, coming up with a list:

SIMILAR
1. Alone.
2. Walked (rode bike) down Elm Street.
3. No blood.
4. Trail went down Spenser's Lane.
5. Dogs stopped in front of old Spenser House, losing scent "in midair," displaying unusual, erratic behavior.

6. Girls and boys.

7. Accompanying items (i.e., bicycle) - some left, some never found.

8. All around age 11.

"It has to have something to do with the old Spenser House," Colton said, stabbing his pencil at that point on the list. "That's where the trail leads then ends, every time."

"But they searched it each time," Marsha argued. "Inside and out. There were no tracks, no dust of years disturbed, no beaten down grass—all boarded and locked up tighter than a jug. They found zilch, nada, nothing around the place."

"I still feel there's a connection," Colton said, shaking his head. "Well, let's put these newspapers up. I'm going to look at the old Spenser House."

"I'm coming, too—" Marsha began, but Colton cut her off.

"No, you go home," he urged.

"But I want to help. She's my little girl!"

"She's *our* little girl," he corrected. "And you're a woman. It's been mostly girls that have disappeared. If there is a sex maniac or sex psycho out there anywhere and if he, or she, were to overpower me, I don't want you anywhere near the place."

"But it was only *little girls,* remember, not grown women!"

"Even so," Colton said. "If this crazy had the opportunity, maybe he'd expand his work to thirty-year-olds. No, you go home. Please. And don't worry about me. I'm tough."

They stood looking at each other for several long seconds before she nodded her head, agreeing to go home. He reached out to her and she went into his arms gladly, knowing the security there.

He stroked her hair, as he used to, years ago.

"Don't worry," he whispered. "If she can be found, if she's alive, I'll do everything humanly possible, and beyond, if necessary, to find her. I have to, you know. I don't want to find out I have a daughter only to lose her this way. It's just not right."

He reached up and brushed away her tears with his fingers.

"Let's get out of here."

Chapter 17

The Lane

Colton left Marsha at Maple and Elm, where he parked the car. She wanted to walk home and he wanted to walk down Elm, slowly, retracing the way the girls would have gone. He wanted to see if he could sense anything.

He knew many people had walked here, searching every square inch of the grass on each side, yet he felt compelled to do it himself.

Nothing happened on Elm, and he paused as he neared the turnoff to Spenser's lane.

This was where one of the bicycles had been found. He turned his back toward The Lane and looked toward the town but, mostly, what he saw was the thick hedgerows. They did not continue on past Elm. At this point, you had to turn either right or left and jog onto one of the other residential streets. All he saw, right or left, were the bushes.

"No wonder no one saw anything," he mused. "Even if people had been in their backyards, they could not have seen anything. I remember these bushes. They have always been this thick."

He was not looking straight into anyone's backyard. These houses had large yards and gardens, so that, actually, the houses were yards away from the beginning of The Lane.

"A perfect spot to grab a little girl and whisk her off down The Lane," he said.

He turned sideways, first to the right and then to the left. There were no houses on The Lane side of Elm. It was really overgrown here at the beginning of the land and down Elm.

Then he made another turn, allowing him to face The Lane and look down it. There was a path down through it. The weeds were thick all the way down The Lane as far as he could see. *So some people still go this way to Number Six,* he thought. *Funny how people forget, or don't care, or new people come along who don't know anything about what's happened here.*

Undoubtedly, hunters till used the path on their way to the deeper woods.

Colton stood still for several minutes at the beginning of The Lane, hoping to feel something, to sense something, to pick up on some sort of "vibes" from this place.

With memories of how he felt years ago flooding over him, fresh on his mind, he thought the same might happen again. He thought about how he had seen an old friend, Louie, act much the same way. Had Louie felt something, also?

What is it about children, he wondered, *especially little girls? Yet some of us, as boys, felt or sensed something wrong here. Chances are there were more than just me who felt something but just didn't say anything to anyone.*

What would they say, anyway? Would they say they had a "funny" feeling, were scared and ran away from this place in panic? They probably wouldn't even remember, anyway, because they wouldn't want to.

"Well, here goes," he said.

Colton took a deep breath and began walking slowly down the single path with a boy's apprehension. He imagined that something might jump out from the sides at him at any moment. He imagined figures and shapes in the shadows of the trees overhead.

Since the electric company had no reason to maintain its line or wires down The Lane, had not had to for years now, they had not trimmed the trees back for as many years.

Some of the branches hung so low over The Lane they nearly touched the top of Colton's head. He imagined snakes on the branches, ready to drop on his head or shoulders as he brushed past.

Stop it, he told himself, firmly. *How can I sense anything if I'm imagining all these things?*

Colton did not pause until he reached the bend that would take him in front of the old Spenser House. He heard nothing but silence and the rustle of leaves and tall grasses in the breeze.

He was far enough away from Midland that he would not have been able to hear the occasional vehicle that might—just might—go down Elm Street, so the silence was eerie, with a preternatural quietness about it.

No animals, large or small, moved in the undergrowth.

Where are the birds? The crickets? he asked himself.

No birds were singing, no crickets rubbing their legs together, making their characteristic chirruping sound.

He had stopped, listening for any sound at all. Now, he made an effort to watch the side of the path, wanting to see some signs of movement in the weeds. He would even have welcomed the sight of a snake, however poisonous, crawling onto The Lane.

The only movement he could detect was the gentle swaying of the tops of the thistles that grew there. Wild daisies swayed lazily, seeming to enjoy the breeze that blew from the south.

Could I be right? he thought. *Has something hap-pened to the animals around here? But what, and what does it have to do with the missing children. Or, does it have* anything *to do with them?*

He took a deep breath, slowly starting around the bend, senses alert for any changes. He came to a stop in front of the house then turned to face it. He didn't realize until he caught his breath that he had been holding it. Then he realized why he had been holding it. He was waiting for the same feeling he had long ago, the same sensation of having the hair stand up on the back of his neck, the feeling of death so near.

But he felt nothing like that.

Was he disappointed? He didn't know if he were or not, couldn't really identify the feeling he did have.

I was only a boy, he thought. *No grown man has the same feelings as when he was young. What did I expect here? There has to be something—this is the spot—right here in front, where all the girls apparently disappeared into thin air.*

Colton unconsciously looked up as he thought that then moved slowly around in a circle, still looking up and around. For a split second, when his back was to the house, he thought he felt something, causing him to whirl around, once more facing the house.

No one. Nothing. Yet he felt like someone, or some-thing, was watching him.

The place was so overgrown, falling down. There

were large gaps in the roof. The roof of the porch was sagging on one side.

Boards still covered the windows and Colton somehow knew they were the same boards that had first been put on there long ago—just more weather-beaten, more warped, the nails rustier.

There were cracks that someone could be looking out of from inside the house.

Colton knew he needed to check the back of the house. Maybe the back door and windows had been broken into and some hobo or vagrant had made the old house home.

He hesitated.

Still that feeling of being watched.

Actually, it was something else rather than being watched. He felt as if something was crawling on his skin, something so gossamer it could hardly be detected, yet sinister in the touch it gave.

Something about the old Spenser House.

What was that little ditty the girls used to sing while jumping rope?

Just

Just don't

Just don't go

Just don't go down

Just don't go down Spenser's

Just don't go down Spenser's Lane

Just don't go down Spenser's Lane by yourself
EVER

Do
Do you
Do you hear
Do you hear me?

He remembered. He could hear their little voices chanting, and see the girls skipping rope. He stood still, hardly breathing, listening. There still were no sounds of life at all. Just a creepy silence. But the sense that all was not right about this place just wouldn't leave him.

The gentle swaying of the leaves of the trees in the summer breeze, the swaying of the knee-length grass in the front yard of the old place belied the ominous feeling about it, a feeling that made Colton shiver, although it was a hot summer day.

What was it? He just couldn't seem to put his finger on it, and he certainly didn't like that feeling.

Telling himself the nervousness he was feeling was caused more by his childhood memories than fear of anyone who might be in the old house, he willed himself to calm down.

Don't panic over what's probably a stupid feeling.

Colton took a step toward the house, then another. A few more steps brought him to the edge of The Lane, opposite the front door of the old house.

He could imagine the Spenser family here, the children playing in the front yard, a swing on the porch, perhaps rocking as Granny Spenser, a famous character around these parts, sat rocking, hulling peas or snapping beans, as most women did in those days. A lot of their work was done outside, either early in the morning—most being up at first light—or late in the evening when it was cool.

For those were the days before air conditioning, when, on many days, the outside was a lot cooler than the inside of the house.

The front porch was big, extending around to the side. There was an old, broken-down swing in the corner hanging by one chain where the porch wrapped around the house. For practical purposes, it effectively cut off the side porch.

He could picture the whole family sleeping out there on cots on nights that would have been too hot and miserable to be indoors.

He'd done it himself as a boy, at a time in this sleepy Arkansas town when no one worried about anyone breaking in or bothering you on the porch during the night. The biggest worry was the mosquitoes, and his family had been lucky enough to have a screened-in porch. And, besides, King, his dog, was always there to protect him.

Now, he saw bits and pieces of rusty screen wire hanging around this porch, relics of lives lived long ago.

He remembered hearing, as a child, that the Spensers

had moved away, even when the house was in its prime, because Granny Spenser had insisted there was an evil spirit in the place.

Were the Spenser boys not harmed, simply because of the fact they were boys, or was it something else?

Colton felt that knowing about the old Spenser House was important. Before he went farther, he decided to find out more. Even when he was a child, the house seemed to be a nice, big, well-built home.

Then why did they *really* leave?

Again, he felt only one person would know.

Old Man Ogden.

Chapter 18

Old Man Ogden

He was still there, sitting in his chair.

"Back again, huh?" he asked, nodding. "Find out anything from the papers?"

Colton shook his head. It sure didn't take people in this town long to know what someone else was doing. It sure hadn't changed in that way.

"Starting to," Colton answered. "But I need to ask you something else, also."

"What that be?" the old man asked, watching Colton closely, as Colton pulled a chair closer and sat down, straddling the chair, the back of the chair facing the old man, so Colton could put his arms on it.

"It's about the old Spenser House. When I was a child, the house was old then, been abandoned for a long time. But, it was obvious, even to a boy, that it had been a beautiful home at one time. So, my question is, why did the Spensers leave it? Could they not find a job, or make a living here, or what?"

The old man had started nodding while Colton was talking.

"You're on the right track all right. She's right about you. Yep, the Spenser House was a humdinger. Just about the fanciest house ever built around these parts when Spenser first built it. There was Spenser and his wife and three children, and, of course, Granny Spenser. She had 'The Sight.'"

"'The Sight'?" Colton asked. What did he mean?

"Yep, had it strong, she did. Her dad had it before her."

"What do you mean?" Colton asked, patiently. He knew not to try to get in a hurry or make the old man rush. He'd find out all he needed to know in time. The problem was that time *was* his problem.

"Couldn't really call her a witch, or sorceress, or anything like that, but she certainly knew things. Could tell you what was going to happen and it usually did. Or, if something had happened, they knew, but they hadn't been told. Granny's dad was beyond my time, of course, but I knew Granny. Let's see..." Old Man Ogden paused, touching his fingers, counting. "Must be nigh onto seventy years I've known her now. 'Course, she seemed old when I was a boy, but she always spoke to me when she saw me. Never spoke to some of the others, just me. At the time, I guessed she liked me more for some reason. Yep, her in that black dress with that black hat with the red flower on it, even in summer…"

Old Man Ogden was watching Colton closely, as if expecting something from him, as he left off speaking, and Colton caught what he was saying.

"Old woman—black dress—black hat with a red flower on it? But you're describing—No, it can't be!" Colton exclaimed. "If you knew Granny Spenser as a boy, and she was old then, then she'd have to be…" Colton stopped, unable to finish his thought, it was so incredible, so unbelievable.

"Dead?" the old man finished for him. "Yep, dead she is, has been for years now, at least according to most folks' reckoning."

He was nodding again.

"What do you mean, according to most folks?" Colton asked. Wasn't dead, *dead*?

"Fact is," continued the old man, "I attended her funeral myself, some years ago, years after they left here. But Spenser brought her back to Midland for burying, being her folks had always lived around here and her parents was buried here. Out to Hilltop Cemetery, they are."

"The old woman I saw two times had a black dress, black hat with a red flower on it," Colton said. "Is that her daughter?"

It had to be her daughter, the other alternative was too unthinkable, somewhere out beyond the realm of reality.

"Granny Smith only had two boys," Ogden replied, shaking his head. "Said when she left there was an evil here, in Midland, and she wouldn't rest until something was done about it, that she hadn't done enough one time when she should have, that she'd do all she could now to kill it. Said someone would come who would figure it out. 'Teren't human,' she said, but it hain't made itself known completely yet, while she was here, so 'twasn't nothing she could do about it before she passed on. But she knew she couldn't rest. She needs to know the evil's been destroyed before her spirit can rest."

Old Man Ogden seemed to be talking to himself, his eyes dreamy and far away.

"What evil?" Colton asked. Then he felt foolish. Here he was asking about impossible things, believing an old man's tale of Granny being "A Diviner" with some special insight and that an old woman's spirit wouldn't rest until some evil was gone from somewhere. No one believed in that sort of thing anymore.

"She's been waiting on you, Young Mitchell. She knows you're the one."

Colton was even more skeptical.

"Are you trying to tell me that an old woman I've seen twice is Granny Spenser, who's actually been dead for many years now, and you know she's been dead, because you went to her funeral?"

"Yep, went to her funeral, myself, I did," the old man said. "Went right up to the casket and saw her lying in it, looking as peaceful as pie, but knowing she weren't resting a bit."

Old Man Ogden nodded.

"Not a bit," he repeated.

"So, now, this is her spirit, or whatever, walking around, trying to find someone to do something about this 'evil' that exists in Midland. Do I have this straight, or have I missed something somewhere?"

Colton knew he was crazy for thinking the old man could help him. If Ogden thought these things, how could Colton believe anything else he said? The guy was loony tunes!

"Yep, she knows you're the one. Felt it myself when you first walked in this morning. You've almost figured it out, just don't know it yet. But she knows you're close, and her spirit's grown stronger with the knowing."

"If you know I've almost figured 'it' out, why haven't you figured 'it' out before now, and done something about it? If you know what it is—why not just tell me? Why all the mystery?"

The old man sighed. "I hain't strong enough, Young Mitchell, and it hain't my purpose in this life."

"Fighting evil isn't your purpose? Why didn't you do something years ago, when the first little girl disappeared? You were younger and stronger then."

"It was not for me to know, that's all. I can't get it,

not all. Something always escapes me. It's not my purpose here," the old man repeated.

Crap! Colton thought. *A Diviner, purposes, spirits. What's going on here? Maybe I did enter* The Twilight Zone.

"All right," he said to the old man. "Can you just tell me where the Spensers live now? I'll talk to them, find out why they really left. Find out if someone else maybe owns the old place now and someone's maybe out there."

"I know why they left. Hain't you been listening? Granny said there was an evil presence in the house, fighting her, and they couldn't stay. Seems she just never could pinpoint it exactly. It wouldn't let her."

"Yes, I heard you," Colton responded to the first part of his statement. "But, still, I'd like to talk to the rest of the family, maybe find out more. It'll let me know more about what to do."

He didn't want to get the old man excited or agitated. He needed to keep him on his side. Colton was afraid if he got him upset or offended him, he might not tell him anymore. And when he wasn't talking about spirits, he seemed to have some good information.

"Parents are dead, Henry and Alma, but the boys still live in Fort Smith, last I heard. At least one does. That's the way it is nowadays. The youngsters move off to the city, first thing you know, they've moved even farther away. Don't seem to care anymore about where they were born, or old neighbors..." His voice trailed off, his head slumping onto his chest.

"And what are their names?" Colton asked.

"Huh?" the old man asked, his head coming up. "Names, you say?"

"Yes, the names of the Spenser boys."

"Let's see, there was George and Seth. Yeah, that's them."

"Thanks, Mr. Ogden," Colton said. He put his hand on the old man's bony shoulder. The old man had shut his eyes, laying his head back on the chair.

Yes, rest, Colton thought.

Chapter 19

Louie

Colton planned not only to try to talk to at least one of the Spensers, but his old friend, Lou, as well. He wanted to know just what had scared Lou that day so long ago.

Colton found his friend's name in the Fort Smith telephone book, the book still hanging from a chain in the only public phone booth in Midland. It was a pleasant surprise to find the book there. He'd been sure he was going to have to call information for the number. Most phone booths had their books ripped off so often the telephone companies no longer put them in the booth.

As the telephone began ringing, Colton thought he

could actually hear the seconds going by. He knew that wasn't so, only that he was acutely aware that every second going by meant he might not find Abigail alive, even if she was at the moment. But until he knew for sure, every second counted.

Just when he thought no one was going to answer, someone picked up the phone and a man's voice answered.

"James residence."

Colton breathed a sigh of relief.

"Louie, thank God you answered."

On the other end, Lou James was startled. No one had called him Louie for more years than he could remember. Not since he was a kid in Midland.

"Who is this?" he asked.

"Louie, it's me. Colton. Colton Mitchell."

"Colton! Colt! How about that? After all these years! What's up, man? It's good to hear from you."

Lou was willing to talk to an old friend, thought the call would just be about old times, maybe they could meet for coffee or lunch or something.

"Maybe you won't think it's so good when you hear what I'm calling about, Louie. It's real important. Do you have a few minutes?"

"Sure, I run my own business here. What's wrong?"

Lou had spotted the anxiety and hurry in Colton's voice and wondered why he would be calling him about something important. Why, they hadn't even seen each other since high school, Lou had not gone to the Class of '64's tenth reunion, which he heard later had really been something. But with a wife like his—

But Colton was speaking, urgently.

"We can get together after this, but right now I need some information from you about something that happened when we were both eleven."

"Eleven! That's awhile back, old friend."

"I know but you've just got to remember."

Lou was already starting to remember being eleven—baseball, swimming, teasing the girls, especially chubby Mary Ann Durmont.

"There was a time," Colton continued, "when you came late to Number Six. The gang was already swimming, including me. Everyone was splashing everyone out in the deep water. For some reason, I had gone up to the shallow end and had climbed upon The Rock. Remember The Rock?"

How could any of them forget The Rock? It was one of the things that made Number Six so special as a swimming hole, that and the ropes tied to the overhanging branches of trees that could be swung out over the water and let go of, dropping the person into the water. What special times!

But The Rock.

So far out in the water, there was a "drop off," but right before the drop off, there was a huge rock, a good three feet square, with the top just below the surface of the water at that point. Countless games of "king of the mountain" were played off that rock. Parents loved it. It kept the children occupied for hours on end while they could swim out in the deep part and enjoy being by themselves for a while.

Races were held with The Rock as the goal. Whoever got there and was able to get up on it, won. It could be used as a resting place, and that was what Colton had decided to do that day—sit on The Rock and rest a minute. If he lay down on it, the water came just to his chin, nothing threatening.

"I had decided to sit on The Rock and rest, one time when everyone was there but you, and then I spotted you. You were up on The Lane, behind that sumac bush by the sycamore tree. You didn't know anyone was watching, Louie, you thought we were all out in the deep part, splashing each other. I only had a minute before someone decided to pull me off The Rock and dunk me. But I saw you, Louie, I saw you."

"Saw me, Colt? What are you talking about?"

But Lou was beginning to suspect what Colton saw that day and a chill began to come over him, the same chill he had that day. Nothing in his life before or since had compared to that feeling. But a chill, anyway, because he was starting to remember and he wasn't sure he wanted to remember. He had safely tucked that day away in his subconscious for many years now. Why would Colten want him to remember? He didn't want to.

"I saw you bent over, bent double, hands on your knees, breathing hard. You were breathing so hard, chest heaving so hard, I thought you were going to throw up and then you did turn away and start to throw up. That's all I saw before Scott grabbed me and pulled me under. I never got a chance to look that way again, but then there you were, in the water. But I saw the look on your face, Louie, and you didn't stay in the water long, claiming you had a stomachache, blaming it on your mom's meat-loaf."

And that was a joke with them all. Lou had started to get mad the first time one of his friends said how awful his mom's meatloaf was, but, since he knew how awful it was, he decided to laugh instead. But still they all had eaten it while at Louie's, out of politeness, if nothing else. And nobody had actually gotten sick from eating it. It just tasted like sawdust, that was all.

But Colton didn't stop.

"But I knew better, Louie. I knew better because I knew why you were standing there heaving, trying to get your breath, and so tired from running that your stomach was cramping so that you had to throw up. You ran all the way from the old Spenser House, didn't you, Louie?"

Yes, yes! Louie wanted to scream. *But shut up. I don't want to remember!*

He didn't say these things to Colton, but he felt them, anyway.

"Louie, I *know* why you ran. Believe me, *I know.* I

really do. And I don't blame you one bit. I ran, too."

Colt ran? Colt, everyone's idol? Had it happened to Colton, also?

"Why didn't you say something, Colt?"

"You know I couldn't do that," he replied softly.

Yes, Lou knew he couldn't have done that, couldn't have said anything to him or to anyone else about what he saw that day. And he would not have asked Lou about it, either. Just as there were unwritten rules of conduct among any group of children, different rules in different places for different groups, so there were unwritten rules within the gang often eleven- and twelve-year-old boys for many years in Midland. One of those unwritten rules was that you never, ever, said or did anything to embarrass or "put down" one of the gang.

No one person in the group, and there were fourteen of them, enough for a baseball team with relief, tried to boss or bully the others. It was that kind of group, just a loyal, fun-loving group of friends, and life was easy and wonderful because there was not a bully on one end or a "ninety-pound weakling" on the other.

Lou remembered, in the craziness of this moment, this crazy remembering moment, that this unwritten rule even went into the classroom when someone made the type of noise they shouldn't have. Or was "full of flatulence," as Mrs. Baker, the fifth-grade teacher, would say. By the time she turned around, even if she knew from what general direction the noise had come, what she saw were serious faces everywhere. Even the girls knew the rules.

What a thing to remember, Louie thought. But it was part of their lives then. They would laugh later on the playground and congratulate the one who had made the noise, especially the loud and smelly ones, but never, ever, was anything said in the classroom.

Never to embarrass any of them or get anyone in trouble. They all liked each other and got along too well for that. Even Mary Ann knew they teased her because they liked her, not to make her feel bad.

"But we need to talk about it now, Louie," Colton was saying, bringing Lou out of his reverie.

"Why? What's going on?" Lou wanted to know what was so important about it now, all these years later.

"I can't explain all of it now, Lou, just trust me with this, okay?"

"Sure," Lou said, without hesitation. He would have trusted his life to Colton when they were boys. He would do the same now.

"What made you run, Louie?"

Lou knew if Colton said it was important, he could force himself to talk about it but he still wasn't sure he wanted to. Almost as if talking about it might make it happen again.

"Colt, we never laughed at each other as children or teenagers growing up. That rule, remember. Well, do you promise not to laugh now? Seriously?" Lou took a deep breath, not waiting for Colton to answer.

"Yes, of course, I promise."

"I was late going to Number Six, as you know. And, being late, I decided to take Spenser's Lane. 'Cause, not only was I late because I had to help Dad, but when I went to get my bike, I had a flat then couldn't find the pump. Dace probably had it somewhere. You remember my brother, Dace. Anyway, being so late, I took The Lane."

And that's the only reason anyone ever took it. The thought came to Colton. *That's the reason I did. No one ever used it otherwise, always going down County Line Road instead.* And they never talked about why they never took it. Was it because of the rule, or was there another reason?

Lou cleared his throat. "Everything was fine at the beginning. I walked along, whistling at the birds, trying to get a response. Nothing much was happening, just a few rabbits in the bushes, maybe mice. I decided as I walked along that I was really going to get a good look at the old house as I walked by, maybe even look at it the whole time I passed by. I felt so big and brave that day— until I got there!"

His voice had lowered, although he probably wasn't aware of it.

Colton waited, giving his old friend time to tell this how he needed to.

"When I first went around the curve, everything was fine. I even got up enough nerve to look over at the old place. I came just about even with the old well, you know where that is."

Colton nodded, as if his friend could see. He knew Lou didn't really expect an answer.

"About that time, it was—was—really creepy. I had heard the expression about hair standing up, but I always thought it was just that—an expression. And what does an eleven-year-old boy from the country know about fear, anyway? But, I swear, really, Colt, the hair actually stood up on the back of my neck. I felt…a…a *presence* of some kind…I remember thinking it was an evil spirit. I felt a cool breeze flow over me. And what did I know about evil spirits? That was only a term, too. Sunday School kept all the evil away from us, right?

"But I knew, I knew in a split second that my life was in danger from this…presence, or whatever it was, and that I was near death, I knew that it was going to kill me. And don't ask how I knew that—some primitive survival instinct in my brain, I guess, was warning me. Anyway, I ran. I ran for my life. I ran faster than I ever had. I probably would have beaten an infield fly to home base, that's how fast I knew I was running. I didn't slow down until I reached the last bend to Number Six. I walked those last few yards, but it didn't help. What you saw was the result of that run. Whether I threw up from the physical exertion or from the fear, I'll never know. I even dropped my towel, and as far as I know, it's still there, rotting in front of the Spenser House. I wasn't about to go back for it, either. Mom threw a fit but I just pretended someone else must have picked it up and told her no one admitted to it. I never asked about it, of course."

Colton couldn't tell, but a shudder went through Lou, with his remembering.

"Does that help you any, whatever this is all about?"

"Yes, yes, it does, Louie. Just one more question. When you felt the presence, did you also hear a voice?"

Lou was silent for a few seconds, thinking, trying to remember.

"I really don't know if it was a voice, exactly. I always thought it was my own brain telling me to run. But I do know the presence came from the old Spenser House."

"And you never said anything about it."

"Now, Colt, you know better than that. We never embarrassed or made fun of anyone under ordinary circumstances, so how could I tell about that? I was afraid of being called a 'fraidy-cat, wimpy…whatever. Besides, as far as I knew, others had walked down Spenser's Lane at various times and never said anything happened. I did wonder, though, many times, if it had happened to anyone else, and they just never said anything, just like me. You, Colt, did it happen to you?" Louie asked, surprised, as if the thought had just come to him. "You said you understood. Did you have the same feeling?"

"I sure did, Lou, but I distinctly heard a voice telling me to run, run for my life. Whether it was in or outside my head, I couldn't say, either."

Both paused, remembering.

Lou spoke first. "Is this something to do with the old Spenser House, Colt? What about it?"

"I don't know, Lou, I really don't. But I called you about this because I'm going to find out."

Or die trying, he added to himself.

"Let me know what you find, okay?"

"Sure will. Thanks, Louie."

They hung up with a promise to get together. Colton didn't have a minute to lose. It was already a little after nine.

He knew what his next step had to be.

Chapter 20

George

Again, Colton was grateful for a small town that left the telephone book in the booth. He was also grateful for a lot of change.

As Colton looked up the name, he hoped there was only one George Spenser in Fort Smith. Surely, Spenser wasn't a common name, not spelled with an S instead of a C. The only George he found was under the name Spencer spelled with a C. And although the spelling was different, he decided to take a chance on it. What did he have to lose at this point?

But wait. How old would George be now? This may not even be the original George, if even the right one.

That George would be….Colton did a quick mental calculation. Good. He would be in his sixties, surely no more.

The phone on the other end was picked up after the third ring.

"Hello?" a man answered.

Bingo. First try. I hope, Colton thought.

"Hello, is this the George Spenser who lived in Midland, back in the 1930s, in a house now called the old Spenser House, down The Lane toward Number Six?"

There was a definite, pregnant silence on the other end of the line.

Oh, no. Colton winced. *Why did I blurt all that out so rapidly? He probably didn't even catch it!*

"I caught what you said," the man's voice answered. "And, yes, I'm that George Spenser, but who wants to know? What's this all about?"

Colton felt as if he'd been slapped. He *knew* he hadn't said that out loud, about not catching it. He *knew* he'd only thought it, yet this man seemed to know what he was thinking.

"Well?" Spenser asked. "This is your nickel, you know."

"Yes," Colton said, startled out of his thoughts. And he was glad to be away from those thoughts. He had started thinking things like "A Diviner" and he didn't want to believe in such things. *Yet, how did he know…*

"Sorry," he said. "My name's Colton Mitchell. I was

born and grew up in Midland, too. I'm doing some research on small towns and decided to start with my own
hometown of Midland. And the old Spenser House seems
to be a central figure in the place, even as I remember it
as a boy." He kept up the story about his research. The
Simmons had believed it, so probably this man would,
too.

"Is that so?" Spenser asked. "I knew an Abe Mitchell. That your dad or kinfolk?"

"Yes, he's my dad," Colton answered. *Yes, they
would be about the same age, give or take.*

"I've wondered what happened to some of my
friends and the people I knew in school there. After we
moved away, we lost contact with everyone there, or
maybe they lost contact with us, whichever way you want
to look at it."

"That's one of the things I want to ask you about,"
Colton said. "Your house seemed like it would have been
a beautiful home back when it was first built. If it isn't
too personal, and you don't mind my asking, why *did* you
move away?"

Again, several seconds went by before the man
spoke. As before, Colton seemed to sense some sort of
reluctance on this man's part to talk, although he could
not imagine why that would be so. People moved around
all the time. Colton was sure Spenser would just say it
was because he did could make better money at the time
in Fort Smith, so they moved.

So, Colton was surprised at the answer Spenser gave, although he later knew he should not have been.

"Well, it was Granny, actually," Spenser began. "Do you remember Granny Spenser, my grandmother?"

"Not really, not personally, for sure, of course," Colton answered. "She was before my time. But I remember folks talking about her occasionally. Only good, of course," he hastened to add.

Spenser chuckled. "That may or may not have been so, especially in her older age. It doesn't matter now, anyway. Granny's been gone for many years now."

Oh, yeah? Colton mused. *What would this man do if I told him she was walking the streets of Midland in the dress and hat she was buried in? He'd think I was crazy, hang up, and refuse to even talk to me again, that's what.*

"How did it happen that she was the reason you moved?" he asked, bringing the conversation back to where he needed it to be.

"Well, how long you got here? Several minutes? 'Cause I'll need to go back several years for you to understand," Spenser asked.

"I've got time," Colton replied, secretly hoping the man could put things simply and quickly. Some people seemed to be able to tell things quickly, others took forever in the telling.

"I know some people never believed that Granny had any special abilities, and her father before her, but you only had to live with her every day for years to know there was certainly *something* about her. And it wasn't just extra instinct or common sense as a lot of people tried to say. Granny knew things, and I started feeling things, too. Granny said at that age I didn't fully have any insight of 'A Diviner' yet, that it would develop with age. She called what I had simply 'knowing things.' But you wanted to know why we moved. One day, we came home from school to find the outer cellar door locked and boarded up and the cellar door to the kitchen locked and sealed. They had put new wallpaper on that wall. If you didn't know what had been there, you couldn't tell. Mom just said Granny had insisted on it.

"And many times I caught Granny looking at me or at Seth with a puzzled frown on her face, like she was trying to remember something, or she would start to say something, but then her face would go blank, and she wouldn't say anything. After a few seconds, she would shake her head and start doing something else. Pretty soon everyone forgot about the boarded up cellar.

"Granny started in about there being an evil presence in the house, and she finally got so bad that Dad decided to move. Granny wanted completely out of the area, so Dad moved to Fort Smith. Granny talked about the evil until the day she died."

Again, Spenser paused. "I loved my Granny and I hated to see her start acting the funny way she did. Just old age, we thought. But she seemed to have lost some of her insight or abilities to sense things as she grew older.

And, as far as I know, mine never developed, even if I ever had it," he added, chuckling. "Does any of this help you?"

"Did you try to sell the house?" Colton asked.

"For years and years. Funny thing, people said it felt 'funny' when they went into it, that they didn't feel comfortable in it, so it never sold. After so many years, Dad just went back down there and boarded up the windows and all. I haven't been back there in more years than I can remember. Is it still standing?"

"Yes, it is," Colton said, and described the place for Spenser.

"We still own it, of course," Spenser said. "Maybe I should try to do something with the land."

"Thanks for your help," Colton said. "That'll add a lot of local color to my story."

"If you ever write it," Spenser said. "But your reasons for wanting to know are your own. I just hope I helped."

Colton quickly said goodbye. He felt Spenser probably had more "insight" than he knew he had. This modern age just didn't believe in such things anymore, so he had not exercised or experimented with his power, and it never developed.

But Colton was starting to wonder about the whole thing.

Chapter 21

Dan

March 1976:

Sheriff Dan White closed the file cabinet with a firm push. He carefully chose a key from his ring and locked the cabinet. He was proud of the way he kept things so organized, just as he was proud of being the youngest sheriff ever elected in South Sebastian County. Of course, he made sure his pride didn't show, having worked with his present staff for several years, as peers, before running for and being elected sheriff.

He needed their support on a professional basis and desired their friendship in his personal life.

"Hey, Kelly, how about helping me clear all that junk off that old desk in the storeroom? I want to move it to my office and use it there."

"Coming, Dan." Kelly, a longtime friend and officer, responded. "Boy, I didn't even know all these years that this old thing was stuck way back in this corner, hidden behind all this junk."

"Me, neither," Dan agreed, starting to lift and remove boxes. "We really need to check and see what all these boxes have in them, too. But we've got the next four years to do that. Right now, I want to get the desk out."

The two men worked steadily for a while, not talking.

"Look at that!" Dan exclaimed, when they had enough boxes and stacks of papers removed to see a good-sized area of the desk.

"Wow!" Kelly said. "What a beauty."

The desk was solid oak, the light golden oak color, an old roll-top, with a top that pulled down. It had brass knobs on the drawers. A row of "pigeon holes" provided spaces for letter or whatever.

"What a find," Dan said. "I'm glad I spotted this. Who stuck it away like this, anyway?"

"I have no idea," Kelly answered. "It's before my time. Frank's been on the force a long time. Let's ask him tomorrow."

"Let's finish and get it into my office."

Before they could remove the desk, they had to rearrange all the boxes and other items. By the time they had pushed, pulled, and exchanged the two desks, it was long past shift change.

Several men had poked their heads into the room, with various comments and offers of help, but the two men wanted to get it done themselves.

"How does that look?" Dan asked, when it was in place against one wall in his office.

"Great. Just like it was meant to be there," Kelly replied.

Dan went over, pulled out a bunch of papers from one of the pigeonholes and started looking through them.

"Hey, how about let's calling it a day and grabbing a pizza and beer?" Kelly asked. "I'm pooped. Can't that wait 'til morning?"

Dan smiled. "You're right, and I'm pretty tired, myself. I'll lock up here and we'll go eat."

Dan took one last look at the old desk as he started to pull his door shut. He was filled with a sense of accomplishment at having discovered the desk and moving it, and, suddenly, he was swept with another feeling also, one he couldn't identify. It was as if the old piece of furniture was about to change his life.

He shivered then shook his head.

What a feeling.

"Yep, it's been around here a long time," Frank said, looking at the desk the next morning.

"Let's see…it was here when I came in 'fifty-five. 'Course, it was old then. Old Sheriff Watkins used it the twelve years he was sheriff, then Sheriff Jones. I guess somewhere along those years, it was moved into the storeroom. I never was in the office much when Jones was sheriff. He had too many radical ideas. Yeah, it must have been along about then," he continued, "'cause Jones bought a lot of new furniture and had the whole place redone."

Dan rubbed his hand over the surface of the desk. "Lots of history in that old thing."

Frank turned away from the office door to answer the phone ringing on his desk.

"Lots of history," Dan repeated to himself. "I can't wait to read these old papers."

He stayed too busy during office hours to even think of the desk, but as soon as his day was over, he sat down at it to go through the holes and drawers, starting with the bundle of letters he had picked out yesterday.

The only interesting thing about some of the letters, mostly receipts for office supplies, were the dates, some going back to the 'fifties.

"Someone will want these stamps."

The contents of the pigeonholes were really pretty ordinary, so Dan went on to the drawers, deciding to open the bottom right one first, then work his way up.

The drawer contained a single item. It was an old accordion-style brown file, the kind with the flap and string that you wound around the little knob, to keep the file closed.

As he unwound the string, he had the same funny feeling he had last night. Ignoring the feeling, he opened the top, reached in, and pulled out a handful of papers. Laying them on his desk, he looked at the top one.

"Carbons," he said to himself. "It has to be old, no one uses carbons anymore, they just make copies on the copier."

He was looking at a copy of an old police report form. The typing was smeared here and there, as if the original sheet had been corrected and the typist had erased the top copy without bothering to erase the carbon and then had re-typed the original. But the words were readable, if just barely.

He found other reports, but only casually glanced at them. Old reports were simply that, just old reports.

But then he came to some old newspaper clippings. They were yellow with age, and the headline caught his eye.

LITTLE GIRL MISSING

He put it down and picked up another, which also announced:

ELEVEN-YEAR-OLD GIRL KIDNAPPED!

After looking at a few more, he began to suspect

there must be a connection, so he went back to the first one he had picked up and read the article about an eleven-year-old girl missing, just disappearing into thin air, or so it seemed from the article.

Then he noticed the town and the date.

Midland.

His uncles and aunt had lived as children in Midland, but he himself had never lived there. In fact, he had never even been there. He had been born in Fort Smith and he grew up there.

In all his seven years with the sheriff's department, he had not been on a single case in Midland. But the name stuck in his mind somehow. What was it?

He leaned back in his chair, relaxing and closing his eyes. This always helped him to think.

His eyes flew open. Now, he remembered. About a year and a half ago, he had been on loan to a county down in South Arkansas, to help them investigate and, fortunately, solve a series of rapes. They caught the guy, which made his record look good. It probably had helped him get elected.

When he returned here, the men were talking about a case, a kidnapped little girl. It wasn't his case, having been assigned while he was away. He didn't hear it discussed much, but he did remember.

That was only two years ago or so.

He looked again at the dates on the other articles in the file and quickly saw by the dates it was every three years—beginning with the year 1957.

The one from two years ago was not in here, the one for 1974.

He wanted to find out something from Frank and dialed his deputy's home number.

"Frank, it's Dan."

"Hi, guy. What's up?"

"Remember today when we were talking about the old desk and who had used it?"

"Yeah, what about it?" Frank asked. He was already home, having been on the early shift for the day.

"Well, I found some old papers in here and I'd like to know how long they've been here. Would you try to remember just exactly when the desk was put back in the storeroom?"

"Um," Frank began. "Let's see…it had to be about ten years ago…" He paused. "Yeah, I'd say around ten years ago. That's about when old Jonesie rearranged everything. What've you got?"

"I'm not sure right now if it's even anything at all. Just something I want to check out. Nothing important, I'm sure. You know how interested I am in old papers, antiques, and junk like that."

Frank laughed. "Yeah, I know. Just don't stick your finger into an old mousetrap!"

Dan laughed, also. "Thanks, Frank, I'll see you Monday."

The next day, Saturday, Dan returned to the office, carrying the old file, which he had taken home with him. He had spent all of the evening and most of the night reading every word of the reports and newspaper articles. Now, he wanted to check old files to see if there were children missing from those other years, 1969 and 1972, and if the sheriff's department had found them or solved the cases.

"Hey, Dan," said one of the men on duty. "It ain't time for reelection yet. You don't have to work *this* hard!"

Dan smiled at the man. "Just some unfinished paperwork," he said.

The man just shook his head at the other officer on duty, returning to his own work.

The reports from two years ago would still be in his file cabinet, while the one from five years back would be in storage boxes in the back room, the room the old desk was in when he found it.

He wanted June or July, two years ago. It didn't take him long. He found the folder and the report of the investigation. There was nothing about it being solved, no kidnapper caught, and the body of the little girl was never recovered.

He pulled it out of the file cabinet, putting it next to the old file on his desk.

They had been in such a hurry to get the desk uncovered, they had not put the storage boxes back in chronological order, so it took him several minutes to locate 1969.

There it was. He found the folder under June, titled under the little girl's name.

He was excited as he walked back to his office. He just knew he was about to discover something, some un-solved case he could sink his teeth into, so to speak. Sometimes the only excitement for the sheriff's depart-ment in this part of the county was chasing down a truck-load of teenagers driving down a country road, knocking mailboxes off their posts with a baseball bat.

After reading the last report and newspaper article, he knew, just knew, he was reading about the same killer. This killer attacked and kidnapped eleven-year-old chil-dren, and they just simply disappeared off the face of the earth, kidnapper and child.

The only connection he could see was a few pieces of evidence left in the same spot, and one particular man questioned each time. The first three times, the mother had given the grown man an alibi, claiming he was with her at home. Still, they released the man after question-ing.

"That's where I start," said Dan, talking to himself, tapping his finger on the man's name in the report. "It's just too much of a coincidence."

❧❧❧

The next morning Dan went to the county judge to

get a warrant to search the home and grounds of a man named Otis Ledbetter, the one name that kept reoccurring in the articles. He took the newspaper clippings and explained his findings. The judge granted him the warrant.

He needed to make one phone call before he left, though.

There were just some people you didn't ignore in this part of the county. You put them in the loop of anything you felt was important.

"Phil Clark here," answered the voice on the other end of the line.

Phil Clark was not only mayor of Midland, but justice of the peace, as well.

"Mr. Clark, hello," Dan began. He explained who he was.

"Yes, Sheriff, I voted for you. How're things going?"

"Just fine, so far. I'm calling you because I've just recently run across some old reports and clippings concerning the disappearances of several children from Midland."

"Oh, you mean the children who've all disappeared several years apart, do you?"

"Yes, that's the ones. I would like to investigate those cases further, especially in reference to one man who they questioned every time. Thought you might know him."

"And who might that be, Sheriff?"

"His name is Otis Ledbetter, and it seems his name

just kept popping up. What can you tell me about him?"

"Well, now, Sheriff, I'd say, in my opinion, you're barking up the wrong tree, there."

"And why is that, Mayor?"

"Well, Otis is what you might call our resident slow learner, if you know what I mean."

"No, Mayor, I'm sorry, but I don't know what you mean. Can you explain it to me?"

Dan fought to keep the control in his voice, knowing that with these country mayors, it didn't help to get them on the defensive. Then you would never get any information from them.

"Well, Otis is what we used to call deaf and dumb, has been since birth. Now we call it developmentally disabled, of course. His mother never sent him to school, saying she could take care of him and he couldn't learn, anyway, being deaf and dumb. Otis can't read or write. Never learned proper sign language, either. Now, I don't know if he's slow 'cause he never had any schooling, or because he was born that way. Just slow, is all I know. 'Course, if you explain some things real slow-like and ask some yes-and-no questions, he can understand some things and answer. He reads lips a lot. You just can't put too much on him at one time, that's all. But if you think he had anything to do with the missing children, then you're wrong. Otis wouldn't hurt a fly. If a young bird falls out of the nest, he puts it back. Used to have all kinds of animals out at his place."

"Used to?" Dan asked.

"Yep, before a plague or something wiped out all the animals around here."

"So, you, personally, don't think this man capable of violence?"

"Nope."

"I'd like to question him, anyway. For one thing, if his mother's passed away, who takes care of him now?"

"Well, he has a friend named Tom who looks in on him regular, buys his groceries, and pays his electric bill for him. Otis gets a social security check and the local bank lets Tom cash it for him, and deposit some of it. Otis walks around town, sometimes, picking up things people have dropped or discarded. Most of the time, though, he just stays by himself and putters around his place."

"And where is his place?" Dan asked.

"It's east on Elm Street, just past Spenser's Lane, on the right. Rundown place. But, Sheriff, I still don't see any need to bother Otis. You'd just upset him. Things out of his routine really stress him."

"Oh? And just how stressed does he get?"

"Now, Sheriff, I know what you're getting at, and it's not like that at all. Otis just sits on his porch and rocks back and forth rapidly for a couple of days 'til he forgets what happened and calms down. Strangers, though, especially stress him."

"You're probably right, Mayor, I just want to check every lead."

"Yep, but I know my townspeople, that's for sure. Been mayor major here for twenty years now. Born here."

"Yes, well, thanks, Mr. Clark. I may call you again on this."

"Anytime, anytime," replied the mayor, "always glad to help."

There's one person out there you don't *know,* Dan thought, as he hung up. *One who likes children. And I plan on finding him and bringing him to trial.*

Chapter 22

Dan and Otis

By Monday afternoon, Dan was heading south toward Midland. In his pocket, he had the necessary search warrant to search this Otis Ledbetter's "place" as the mayor had called it.

Armed with the old reports and newspaper clippings, he felt he had enough information to officially reopen the case and search for further evidence.

Now to find Elm Street, then Spenser's Lane, he thought, as he approached the turnoff from the state highway onto Midland's main street.

"So this is Midland," he said, as he drove slowly down the street. He didn't drive slowly, worried about getting a ticket—this small town had no police force and was unincorporated as a town. Perhaps, once, it had been a thriving, populous place, but no more.

His patrol car drew its share of curious stares as he drove down one street then up another. There were so few streets in Midland he knew he had to come to Elm sooner or later.

Oh, here it was, finally. He turned left, or east, on to the street. He drove past an old, overgrown road on his right then an old boarding house with several outbuildings, equally as old, before he realized he must have driven past Spenser's Lane and the Ledbetter place.

It certainly had been a lane, all right. There was no way it you could call it a road, definitely not a street.

After driving back and forth several times, he succeeded in getting his car heading back the way he had come. As he neared the Ledbetter place, he radioed in, giving the exact location where he was.

Dan pulled into the cleared, hard-packed dirt space in front of the house. It was not so defined that you could call it a driveway, just a wide dirt space in front of the house, parallel with the street. He had thrown a quick glance at this place, as he drove by a few minutes before, and had thought what a junk heap it was. Now he got a good look at it.

The house itself was small, old, made of boards that perhaps had been painted white once, but only once and long ago. It had a porch the length of the front, but the roof on one end of the porch was beginning to sag. He shook his head. However much social security this man did or didn't receive, it evidently wasn't enough to cover home repairs.

There were two doors and two windows across the front. This was probably a four-room house, and might or might not contain a bathroom. Some of these old houses out in the country still used wells for water and had out-houses.

Surprisingly, the grass on the small front yard and down both sides of the house was mowed. The area around the outbuildings was cleaned up and relatively clear, but there were some boxes and boards lying against the sides of the sheds. There was a variety of items, large and small, stacked around the sheds.

The outbuildings consisted of a small garage, no door, but no vehicle inside, and two sheds. All the build-ings were made of the same material as the house and were just as old. They all had tin roofs.

Guess he has a friend that helps him keep it mowed, Dan thought, *but not completely picked up.*

On a cursory look, Dan spotted old tubs, pots, and pans, various piles of lumber and boards, tin cans, glass canning jars, and old toys. But although there were many piles of "junk," there seemed to be a certain order to them, as if they were organized in some weird fashion. The whole scene had such a surreal quality to it that Dan thought he had stepped in a Dali painting by mistake.

Dan emerged from his car slowly, carefully, his gun handy. You just never knew what to expect. Some people out here valued their privacy so much, the first thing you might see could be the barrel of a shotgun sticking out a window, aimed straight at you and ready to shoot.

"Hello, the house!" he shouted, not willing to go any closer and surprise anyone.

Now, that was stupid of me, he thought. *I forgot this man was deaf.*

He slowly walked toward the porch. He wanted to check around outside before going into the house itself. Maybe the man would see him through a window and come out. As he walked between the house and the garage, he heard sounds coming from the back of the garage, between that and the first shed.

As he rounded the corner of the garage, he saw a man standing in front of a line of cages. The man was in the process of bringing a rabbit out of a cage.

Dan walked up to the man and touched his shoulder, causing Otis to jump violently. He nearly dropped the rabbit he had been holding and petting.

Otis turned around, his eyes huge in his face, a frightened expression on his face. He took a step backward, bringing his back up against the rabbit hutch.

The rabbit sensed the change in the man and started squirming, trying to get out of Otis's tight grip.

Dan quickly pointed to the rabbit and then gestured toward the cages.

Otis understood what he wanted. He turned and put his rabbit back into the cage. He still had the scared look on his face when he turned around to face Dan.

Of course, Dan thought. *He's faced enough men dressed like me over the years that he's afraid. It probably scared his mother to be questioned and he sensed that, also.*

Dan held up his hand, trying to show this man that he meant him no harm.

"Please, I won't hurt you," he told him, slowly, hoping he would read his lips, like the mayor had said. "It's okay."

Otis started shaking his head from side to side, trembling.

It made Dan wonder what the mother must have taught her son about police officers. This wasn't just a simple respect for the authority the uniform represented. Most people slowed down, stopped doing what they were doing to an extent, whenever they saw an officer or a patrol car, but this was sheer fright at his presence.

Dan pointed to himself then to the warrant he had taken out of his pocket then around at the house and the buildings. He touched his eyes and pointed, trying to show the man he was going to look around.

Otis still had not moved, still had not taken his eyes off Dan. Dan decided just to leave Otis where he was and start looking in the garage first.

The garage had shelves on three sides, and these

shelves were piled high with cans and jars of screws and nails, pieces of old tools, and some old tools themselves. By the look of them, they had not been used in years. Probably the husband and father had used them when he was alive, and that was over thirty-three years ago now. Dan had heard that the husband, Otis's father, had committed suicide on the day Otis was born. That was curious. Usually, the birth of a child was a joyful time, not depressing.

Certain tools were hanging from nails and hooks on the walls, however, and these had the look of use about them—a hand saw, a hammer, and a chisel. Bigger things like a scythe, hoes, and a rake hung from nails sticking out from the boards. These Otis probably used to keep the brush from taking over the place.

Dan had spotted a garden patch. Knowing her son might have to care for himself one day, the mother had probably taught him how to grow the food he would need. Dan suspected the rabbits might be both pets and a food supply.

Across the rafters overhead, there laid a door, several boards, an old bicycle, and an old wooden ladder.

The floor of the garage was simply hard-packed earth. The builders had seen no need to put a floor in the garage. Worn ruts indicated a vehicle had once parked here on a steady basis. Again, though, probably when the husband was living. There was no evidence of recent use.

Dan thought he wouldn't be surprised if he found out

later that the local general store he passed on his way through town didn't still deliver groceries. A lot of these older women never learned to drive, being completely dependent on their husbands to provide for them. The local store probably delivered to the woman while she was alive, then to Otis, if needed.

Dan found nothing out of the ordinary in the garage, even though he moved quite a few items around that were stacked under the counter and on top of each other.

Just junk, at least in his opinion.

This man was a true "pack rat."

As Dan turned away from the garage to go to the first shed, he wondered if the man had ever thrown anything away. He wondered if maybe he even purposely collected this stuff. After opening the door, he saw that this shed was so piled up, he wasn't sure where or how to begin looking through it.

He stood still, listening. When he had come out of the garage, Otis was sitting in a rocking chair on the front porch of the house, rocking back and forth, nodding all the while.

Completely stressed out.

Dan could hear him still rocking back and forth— thump, thump—a steady rhythm. Good. If he stayed there, he wouldn't be in Dan's way. Dan also wouldn't look up to a shotgun in his face. He had no desire to, and it had not been his intention to, upset or stress the poor man, but he did intend to do a thorough job of searching this place. He wasn't sure what, if anything, he hoped to find. He did recall reading about the few items of the children that were mentioned in the newspaper articles, these being the few things they had found at the time each disappearance was investigated.

He had not taken the time, so far, to look for any physical evidence in any of the cases, but he knew a room in the back of the building contained lots of boxes with dates on them. If anything looked suspicious here, he would certainly check those.

Dan decided to simply start on the left side of the shed, moving everything on shelves, checking every-thing, and systematically moving around the building in a clockwise fashion. Of course, in order to get to the shelves at times, he would have to move boxes out of the way, looking in them at the same time.

He was halfway across the shelves, on the backside of the shed, when he moved a box of old comic books out of the way and spotted what he was really hoping he wouldn't. There, sitting on the back of the shelf, was a child's lunch box, the old metal kind with the metal clasp on the front, the handle broken off. This box was red and yellow, with a picture of Barbie on it. A Barbie doll lunch box of this kind meant one thing, a date of 1959 or there-about. The Barbies had come out around 1959.

One little girl had her Barbie lunch box in the basket on her bicycle the day she had disappeared, and it was never found. Dan was so excited by his discovery he couldn't remember which girl, or which date, it was. Was it 1960 or 1963?

He took his handkerchief and reached in to remove the lunch box then stopped. He decided to leave it there in the spot it had been in for so long, until he could call for assistance and to have someone as a witness to his find.

He walked to his car and made the necessary call. It would probably take a deputy at least forty-five minutes to get there. In the meantime, Dan could continue his search.

Otis still sat on the porch, rocking back and forth.

Dan was just at the end of searching the first shed when he heard a vehicle pulling in at the front of the house.

He met Frank halfway across the yard. Dan took his deputy to the shed, showed him the lunch box, and they secured it as evidence.

"What's going on here, Dan?" Frank asked, looking around. "What're you working on?"

"Remember the cases of the children?" Dan asked.

"Well, sure, but you don't think this guy has anything to do with them, do you?"

"Why not?" Dan asked. "You just saw one of the missing items one of the little girls had when she was last seen. I wanted a witness to the fact that it had been in this shed a long time."

"Excuse me, Dan, but this guy's mentally handicapped, really slow. He probably didn't have anything to do it, and he was questioned at the time. He was released."

"Well, that's for us to find out. Sometimes, even in their limitations, persons with disabilities know and do a lot more than we give them credit for, or don't give them credit for, whichever way you want to look at it."

Frank shrugged. "Maybe so. He can always be tested, like you say. You said something about looking further."

"Yeah," Dan answered. "I haven't made it to that last shed yet. Is Otis still on the porch? I don't want any surprises."

They stopped to listen and heard the "thump, thump" of the rocker. Otis was now making whimpering sounds.

Dan and Frank looked at each other, Frank raising his eyebrows.

"Seems two of us really upset him," Dan said.

"How so?" Frank asked.

"Well, I was told by the mayor here how Otis goes to his rocker and rocks whenever he's upset. He's been doing that ever since I've been here, but you've made him make sounds, also.

"He can't talk?" Frank asked.

"No, he's deaf, mute, with limited mental capacity."

Frank shook his head again. He still had his doubts.

"And you seriously think this guy has something to do with kidnapping those children?"

"Don't you think it's possible?" Dan asked. "He's a strong adult, was adult age when the first one disappeared. His body would react as any adult male, he would have the same needs. Problem is, the mayor told me, that by the next day, he never remembers what upset him the day before. He doesn't even remember anything happened the day before, or at least pretends not to. Hell, he could have done anything to those little girls at the time and not even know it now."

"Well, there have been cases of those with limited abilities doing atrocities to children, boys and girls. They simply end up in mental institutions for the rest of their lives," Frank mused. "Stranger things have happened. And here *is* the lunch box."

They opened the door to the other shed, the one at the back. It was as piled up as the garage and other shed had been. As before, Dan decided to start just to the left of the door and systematically search the place.

"One question," Frank said, as they started. "Just exactly what are we looking for here? Another lunch box?"

"No, but there could be articles of clothing, for one thing. According to one of the newspaper articles, one girl lost a tennis shoe in Spenser's Lane, and they only found one. The other one they never found. Just look for anything that might belong to a child."

The only sounds that they heard for quite a while were boxes and other items they moved around on the shelves. Both men made comments like "would you look at this" and "I can't believe this," but the articles they found were not articles associated with children, just some collector's items.

They were so dusty and dirty that both men sneezed frequently.

"What a pack rat!" Frank exclaimed one time. "Where did he come up with all this junk?"

"As I understand it, he looks around people's trash cans and picks up items from the streets. I wouldn't be surprised if they didn't make regular trips to the local landfill when the father was alive."

"Whoa!" Frank exclaimed, "what's this?" He held up a tennis shoe, the size a little girl would wear. It was definitely old. "You said the article said one tennis shoe was found and one was missing?" he asked Dan.

"Sure did. Let's see it."

Dan moved over next to Frank, taking the shoe. Both men had on plastic gloves, but Dan still took it as gingerly as possible. "Let's take it," he said. "It might be important. I can't tell if it matches the other just by looking at it right now, but it looks close. Let's look around for the mate, though, just in case it's here."

They found nothing else in the shed, however.

They had succeeded in disturbing a mother mouse and a nest of baby mice, uncovering numerous piles of "miller" bugs and scattering many roaches.

After straightening up the best they could, they secured the shed door.

They were halfway to Frank's car to put the items in the truck when another car pulled up, hardly finding room in the cleared space with the two patrol cars.

Dan and Frank stopped, waiting to see who this was.

A man about Otis's age got out, looking hard at Dan and Frank, but going directly to Otis on the porch.

The two men heard the man talking to Otis and, when they came around the house, he was patting Otis's shoulder, trying to calm him down. He succeeded to the extent that Otis stopped hitting the arms of the rocking chair with his hands fisted, but he kept rocking, gripping the handles.

He heard Dan and Frank approaching the porch.

"What's going on here?" asked the man.

"I'm Sheriff Dan White and this is my deputy, Frank. We're here on official business. May I ask who you are, please?"

"Name's Tom Smith. I'm Otis's friend. I've helped look after him ever since his mom passed away."

"You live here?" asked Dan.

"No, on down the road." He pointed as he spoke. "I'm married but I come to check on Otis every chance I get, a couple of times a day, at least. You still haven't said why you're here."

"Are you legally responsible for Mr. Ledbetter?" Dan asked. He wasn't going to answer the man's question until he was ready to, if at all.

"No, just a friend who cares. He needs someone to

look after him, you know. He's not able to do some things for himself. Some, he can."

Tom grew silent, waiting. He looked at the lunch box in Frank's hand and the shoe in Dan's.

Trained to watch people's reactions, Dan could detect no recognition of these items in Tom's eyes. He probably had never seen them before.

"Do you have a search warrant for this?" Tom asked, pointing at the items.

"Why do you assume these came from here?" Dan asked. "Do you think there's something here we need a search warrant for?" He watched the man's face for any sign that might give something away.

They read nothing suspicious in Tom's expression.

"I have no idea what this is all about. And, yes, that lunch box and shoe could very well be something that Otis picked up somewhere. But I do know you need a warrant to look around someone's place."

"As a matter of fact, we do have a warrant," Dan replied, producing the paper.

He handed it to the man, who read it and handed it back.

"Am I right?" Tom asked. "Before the judge signed this, you had to have reason to believe you would find something to do with a crime?"

Dan smiled. People watched too much TV these days. "Yes, sir, you're right."

"Otis hasn't done anything. He's not capable of doing anything wrong or bad. What do you think he's done?"

Dan and Frank looked at each other, wondering how much to reveal. Dan made a quick decision. "I'm sorry, Mr. Smith, we're not at liberty to say what we're investigating at this point, at least not to anyone not related to Mr. Ledbetter. But we would like to advise Mr. Ledbetter not to leave the premises from this time on, until our investigation is complete."

"Not leave?" Tom asked, incredulously. "Are you kidding? He hasn't left this place in thirty-seven years. I don't suppose he's going anywhere now. And he's very upset. What have you done to him?"

"Mr. Smith, we haven't done anything to Mr. Ledbetter. As soon as he saw me, he went straight to the front porch, sat down in the rocker, and has been rocking ever since. I told him who I was, showed him the search warrant, and explained that I would be looking around the place. None of his rights have been violated. I understand he exhibits this kind of behavior when he's upset."

"Yes, he does, that's why I wondered what upset him."

"Only my presence, Mr. Smith," Dan said. "And I assure you I had no intention of upsetting him. I had no control over that. Please believe that we are here on official business, which at this particular point is almost over, although we may be back. Good afternoon, Mr. Ledbetter, Mr. Smith," Dan said, as both men touched their hats and turned to go. They moved back around the house. They wanted to search through the sheds very thorough-ly.

Tom watched both men leave, an uneasy feeling flooding over him. He feared for his old friend, who had no ability to defend himself for any reason.

When they returned to the office, they found the evidence boxes from the years 1957 and 1960, and other items identified as that from the case of the missing children.

"Let's see if that tennis shoe is in one of these boxes, the one they said they found at the time," Dan said.

After looking through several boxes, they found the tennis shoe they were looking for. It was very dusty and faded, but they recognized it. It was the identical match to the one they had found in Otis's shed, in a plastic bag marked with the name, date, and case number. Of course, they would send both shoes to experts to verify the match. But just by looking, there was really no doubt. They also found a broken medal handle, which they felt sure would match the lunch box found at the scene of one of disappearances.

Strangely, the discoveries held no joy for Dan. Because now, the questions started. If this man kidnapped the children, where were the bodies? They would have to search every inch of Ledbetter's place, even digging up everything.

The next day, Dan and a deputy stopped by Tom

Smith's house, requesting the man to accompany them to Ledbetter's house. They not only wanted him as a witness to their actions, but maybe he could keep Otis calm.

Otis was sitting on the front steps of his porch when the two vehicles pulled in.

He stood up, watching Tom as they approached.

. Dan told Otis he was under arrest for the kidnapping of three of the girls, the three they had evidence on. He read him his rights and produced handcuffs to take Otis away.

Otis started trembling and his friend helped him to the patrol car, assuring him he could take care of his rabbits and everything would be okay.

Tom stood with tears in his eyes as the car took off. He could only pray that everything would work out for Otis. He knew his old friend was innocent, but that didn't always matter in a case like this.

So he was afraid.

Chapter 23

Granny Spenser Comes to Dan

an woke with a scream, rising up in bed, his eyes flying open. The blanket fell away, revealing his chest, wet with sweat like his forehead, yet Dan felt a chill.

He shivered.

He couldn't be awake yet, not quite yet.

Standing at the foot of his bed was a figure. Although it was in the shadows, there was enough moonlight filtering through the windows to let Dan identify this figure as the same one that had just come to him in his dreams.

There was a preternatural aura about the figure, an ethereal quality that indicated form without substance, yet

Dan could not see through it. His mind told him what was on the dresser across from him, but the figure blocked the view, as it did part of the dresser itself.

Dressed in black, the little old lady stood deathly still, but her eyes blazed brightly.

Dan caught a glimmer from them as a breeze through the window billowed the sheer curtains outward and moonlight fell across the old woman's face.

"Wha—" Dan began, but stopped when the figure moved.

It was only a whisper of a move, but move it did.

"Help him," the specter breathed, barely audible, yet strangely distinct. The voice seemed to come from another place, another time.

"What?" Dan asked again. It seemed to him he had lost control of his motor senses, unable to move except for speaking that one word.

As he stared at the ghostly figure, a song popped into his mind, chanted in the singsong way of children…

Just

Just don't

Just don't go

Just don't go down

Just don't go down Spenser's

Just don't go down Spenser's Lane by yourself

EVER

Do

Do you
Do you hear
Do you hear me?

Crazy!

Suddenly, he moved, turning sideways and reaching for his revolver, which he kept on the nightstand beside his bed.

Although reaching for and retrieving his gun took less than a few seconds, when he twirled around again, the figure was gone.

A quick look around the room revealed nothing, yet Dan took his time getting out of bed, straining to listen for any telltale sound of movement in the room.

He carefully, and with deliberate motions, moved the bed covers aside. He made sure his legs and feet were completely clear. He wanted total mobility if a figure suddenly jumped out of the shadows at him.

When nothing in the room moved, except the billowing curtains, he slowly lowered his legs. He quickly stepped away from the bed. Again, he wanted no surprises. He knew it only took him seconds to grab his gun. The person had no time to leave the room, or even hide.

What person? he asked himself.

It was only a dream, wasn't it?

Dan shivered again, a rippling going over his body.

Somebody's walking over my grave, he thought, recalling an old saying he had been told from childhood.

He was cold, although it was July and a warm breeze came in through the windows. He glanced at his clock, one with large digital numbers, and discovered it was one-forty-three a.m.

Cautiously, he walked through the room to the door, stepping out quickly with both hands on his gun, turning right, and then left as his training dictated.

Nothing in the short hall.

A rapid inspection of his apartment revealed nothing, as he suspected. He sat down at the kitchen table and found himself shaking. Never before had he dreamed in such a vivid, real-life way. And not only did the woman speak to him in his dream, "Help him," but also said the same thing later, appearing in what he thought was an awakened state, but obviously still part of his dream.

He shook his head. "I just wasn't awake, that's all," he reasoned. "I only awoke when I reached for my gun, and, of course, nothing was there."

He returned to the bedroom.

He didn't fall asleep for a long time, listening to the beat of his heart and the curtains gently billowing with the breeze. He wondered what it meant.

He knew he had been awake.

Chapter 24

Dan and George

The date of the competency hearing for Otis Ledbetter was set for March fifteenth. Because of his limited abilities, they were to determine if he could even stand trial.

Although some people felt if you were responsible enough to commit the crime, you should be responsible enough to stand trial for it, Dan had enough experience to know that was not always the case. Ledbetter was determined competent enough to stand trial, although there had been many protests, including his friend, Tom, who insisted Otis would not be able to understand or answer questions intelligently. Because he was used to communicating with Otis, Tom Smith was requested by the Court to be present at the trial, as much as an interpreter as anything else.

In the meantime, the search for more evidence would continue. A team of deputies and auxiliary police had dug in every possible spot around the Ledbetter home, without results. The main body of evidence from the state would be the lunch box, blue barrette, matching tennis shoe, and matching items found in Otis's sheds, former sheriff employees who conducted the original searches at the time, and opportunity.

Opportunity. What a concept, Dan thought.

This case, involving the two cases, actually, had been utmost on Dan's mind for months now. He looked again, as he had many, many times, at the list of evidence, and he realized that most of the evidence came from old newspaper clippings published at the time.

The prosecution would also be calling in eyewitnesses from both investigations, including the now retired Sheriff Jones. Sheriff Watkins had passed away several years back.

These two men had led the search parties at the time, and, in addition to old written reports, Sheriff Jones could testify as to what was found at the scenes at the time. In one case, a footprint on the south side of Spenser's Lane had been clearly photographed. Sheriff Jones would testify that, at the time, the footprint matched that of Otis Ledbetter.

However, given the proximity of Otis's house to that of the place where the dogs stopped in front of the old Spenser House, it was deemed circumstantial at the time. Each time there not been enough evidence to even arrest Ledbetter, especially since his mother swore he was at home with her during the times of the disappearances.

"Reasonable doubt" came into play.

The reopening of the two cases, and the arrest of Otis Ledbetter, made headline news in the Fort Smith paper, the *Southwest Times-Record*. The local TV, Channel 5, featured it in a broadcast.

Rekindling old memories and feelings made the friends and relatives of the missing children so upset, even after so long a time, that Dan was afraid this whole thing might simply turn into a witch hunt. If *someone* could be blamed and punished for these kidnappings, then everyone felt better. That just seemed to be human nature. Never mind, sometimes, if it were the right person or not!

The not knowing what happened, in any situation like this, or by whom, seemed to prey on people's minds, leaving unsettled and unfulfilled emotions.

If they could find and convict a scapegoat, it eased the emotions.

‿✧‿

As a regular practice, George Spencer tuned into the

ten p.m. local news every evening. Problem was, his TV set had been on the blink and in the shop for the last two weeks, and he hated trying to read a newspaper. He had relied on his wife to tell him what was going on in the world.

The first time he got his own TV back, late on a Friday afternoon, he was ready to watch and listen.

And after hearing the news, he immediately called his nephew.

"Hey, Uncle George, what's happening with you and Aunt Mary?" Dan asked.

George was his favorite uncle, and they really didn't see enough of each other. But he had never called this late at night. Dan figured something must have happened to someone in the family.

"Actually, Dan, I'm calling about this thing I heard on the news just now about those missing girls in Midland, how they seemed to disappear in front of the old Spenser House. This is the first time I heard that the cases have been reopened. What's going on?"

"Isn't that something?" Dan responded. "I have reason to believe we've caught the guy who's been doing it all these years. Of course, we only have evidence, proof even, for two of the cases, so that's all we can bring him to trial for."

"Dan, it *wasn't* Otis Ledbetter," his uncle said, emphatically. "Didn't anyone in the family ever tell you about that house? That's where we were all born and lived as kids. Granny Spenser was the one who insisted we move, insisting there was an evil presence there."

Dan was silent, not knowing what to say in response.

"You're kidding," he said after a long moment. He couldn't believe it. "But your name, as was Mom's, are spelled with a C. In all the articles I've read, the Spenser is spelled with an S."

"Our name wasn't always spelled with a C, and it's not legally now, if you could see our birth certificates. Dad changed it when we came to Fort Smith. Again, because Granny insisted."

"Granny? Who's this Granny you keep talking about?" Dan asked.

But he really didn't have to ask. He knew. Somehow, he knew. How he knew, he didn't know. He just knew.

"She was our grandmother, your great-grandmother," George said. "But about the house. Well, it wasn't only us, it seems. Other people always said they had funny feelings about the place, scary feelings. Granny was still alive when the first two children disappeared. She kept insisting it was because of the evil in the house, that the evil had 'taken' the children.

"As Seth, Hazel, and I grew older, we just decided Granny was as crazy as a bat. Dad said her last words were something like 'it must be destroyed, kill it, kill it.'"

"'It'?" asked Dan.

"Yeah, 'it,'" replied his uncle. "Weird, huh?"

"I'll say, but what does all this have to do with Otis

Ledbetter? We have certain evidence that points to him. Besides, the old house was inspected after each disappearance and nothing was found."

"I just wanted to let you know that none of us, your family, that is, believes that Otis did it. It has something to do with the house. Seth and I used to joke around about how maybe the house just opened up and swallowed the kids who wandered too close to it. Haven't you ever felt anything when you're near it?"

"I haven't actually been near it yet but I plan on going. We're investigating every angle. I don't want any surprises when the trial comes."

"Usually, at least one person in each generation has had 'The Sight,' as Granny called it."

"'The Sight '?" Dan asked.

He now felt totally lost in the conversation.

"Yes, the ability to know things are going to happen, or sense things. Some of us have been wondering about you."

"Sorry, Uncle George, I haven't had any weird feelings or anything like that." Dan wondered why he had lied to his uncle. What was the dream, the vision, or whatever, during the night, if not weird? He insisted to himself that it was just that—a dream.

"Well, I just wanted you to know it's not Otis, that's all."

"Sure. Well—thanks, Uncle George."

Dan hung up and just sat there, his hand still on the

telephone. What a strange conversation, just out of the blue like that. And to find out his family had lived in that old house, the only ones to have ever lived there.

He shook his head.

The trial started tomorrow. At this point, he didn't personally have time to go to the old house. Since Frank and several other deputies had not found anything on further investigation, he decided his uncle was as crazy as his newly discovered Granny Spenser had been.

He wasn't superstitious. He didn't believe in old wives' tales, witches, or stories of hauntings of old houses.

At least he didn't right now.

But the dream…

Chapter 25

Dan Has Doubts

Dan wasn't pleased with the way things were going with the Otis Ledbetter trial. In fact, the more he was around the whole thing, the less pleased he was. Something wasn't right.

Just a feeling he had.

First of all, there was Ledbetter himself. Otis's friend, Tom, was always with him, leading him around. Dan watched them in the courtroom and also in the halls. Otis would cup his hand and tip it to his mouth and Tom would get him a drink. Otis touched his mouth and Tom provided him with a snack. Otis touched his belt and Tom would take him to the bathroom.

Dan was sure this was part of a sign language system, that his mother must have developed with Otis, and Tom learned it over the years so he could communicate with and help Otis. Dan thought how fortunate Otis was to have a friend like Tom.

As Dan undressed for bed late on this Friday night, he was still halfway convinced that Otis's name turning up in every case was not coincidence.

Yet, the more he saw, the more he began to doubt.

He just wasn't sure how he felt. At first, he had felt this man was capable of kidnapping children, possibly of murder, now he just wasn't sure. He had been told about the children riding by Otis's house on their bicycles, waving and smiling at him, and he had thought perhaps that had given Otis the "in" he needed to get near the children, children who had begun to trust him because they felt they knew him from riding by.

Originally, Dan thought that Otis must have used that trust to lure the children to the deserted stretch of road in front of the old Spenser House. Then perhaps at that point, actually, literally picked the children up in his arms, those strong arms, either first knocking them out some way, or the children went with him willingly, thinking they were playing a game. That would account for the fact that the children's footprints stopped suddenly, and the dogs lost the scent "in midair" as it was reported.

If Otis had picked them up there, then naturally their scent would end and the dogs would stop in frustration.

And, then, there was the fact that no bodies had been found, not even bones. Of course, if graves had been dug deep enough, there would be no way of detecting where they would be after all this time. After all, it was now twenty years since the first little girl had disappeared.

Parents of the missing children had been questioned, and they all had ruled out Otis as a suspect. They had considered Otis only friendly and harmless all his life. Indeed, there had been an almost protective, proprietary attitude in their feelings toward him. Not one had expressed any doubts or qualms about him. They had been aware that their children waved to him, and it had not worried them at all.

Could everybody be wrong?

Well, yes—other cases of someone seeming to be a "best neighbor" had proven people could be wrong in their judgment of character, or what people thought others to be potentially capable of doing. But Dan still had the feeling that something was not quite right. He just couldn't put his finger on what it was.

Maybe the clincher in thinking he could be wrong was the fact that Otis had no earthly idea what was going on around him in the courtroom. He had no idea he was being tried for kidnappings and murder. There was a possibility he didn't even understand the concept of kidnapping or murder.

Dan wasn't sure what the court had been thinking at the competency hearing to come up with the conclusion that Otis was capable of standing trial. Of course, they had not observed him then as much as Dan had now.

What Otis did understand was that his lifelong routine had been interrupted—a routine that had provided security for all his thirty-seven years. He sat in the courtroom and rocked his body back and forth, just as he did in the rocking chair on his front porch. He felt the stress of being around strangers and in a strange environment. The only thing helping him stay halfway calm was the presence of his friend, Tom, who they allowed to sit next to him.

Dan knew they were getting ready to condemn this man, and Dan had started it, so sure of himself then, and so ready to make a name for himself.

But this man wouldn't survive in prison.

But what could be done now?

Chapter 26

George

June 1976:

When George hung up the phone after talking with Colton, he allowed his hand to rest on the receiver. What a strange call. Right out of the blue and about the same thing he had just called his nephew about the night before, the disappearance in Midland of all those children. If the man had just driven down from Chicago as he said he had, then he had not seen the local papers, knew nothing of what was going on with the trial and all.

George couldn't decide whether to call Dan, or not.

If Dan had caught the killer, then nothing would come of this Colton person, and there was no need stressing Dan at this particular time. But, on the other hand, if Colton had unearthed some vital information about the case, then Dan needed to know.

He finally decided to give Dan a call.

Dan was not at the office, and his home number did not answer. Since George needed to mow his lawn, he would call later. After all, the trial didn't continue until Monday. He had plenty of time to talk to his nephew.

Dan went to the office in deep thought. He was thinking so hard about this case that it did not register at first that his on-duty deputy was speaking to him. He shook his head. "What? Sorry, what did you say?" he asked.

"You okay, Sheriff? You haven't heard a word I've said."

"I'm okay, just thinking. Did you say something about 'uncle'?" he asked.

"Yes, I said your Uncle George has called here twice for you this morning, once earlier, now about an hour ago. Said he needs to talk to you, to call him at home."

"That's unusual. Did he say what he was calling about?"

"Nope. Just to call."

"Thanks."

Dan shook his head as he walked into his office. His uncle called twice for him in one morning, once last night—an uncle that he, perhaps, talked to once every few months. Now, he got two calls after talking to him this morning. What was going on?

His uncle answered before the first ring had finished. What was he doing, sitting on the phone?

"George? What's going on? You trying to reach me?"

"Yes, Dan. I thought I'd better call you about something that happened this morning since you called me. First, is there anything going on in Midland this morning about this Ledbetter case? Do you have an undercover man there, or something?"

"Undercover man? In Midland?" Dan was surprised. "What would I have an undercover man for? What is this?"

"Well, I got a call from a man, from Midland, who said he was investigating the disappearance of those missing children and asked if I happened to be kin to the Spensers of the old Spenser House, although my name was spelled differently. He was trying to locate them. I had to confess I was. He wanted to know why we had abandoned a perfectly good house, all about it, so I told him about Granny Spenser. He asked a lot of questions, like he knew what he was talking about, and I ended up telling him about our childhood there. He sounded so official I figured he was one of yours."

"No, not mine, but this is interesting. Was he, maybe, working for the prosecution?"

"Don't think so. Said he'd just driven down from Chicago, which I figured was just a story. But he never mentioned the trial, so I'm not so sure he even knew about it, thinking back. Thought I'd better let you know."

"Well, I'm glad you did. I'll check it out right away."

"Oh, Dan—" his uncle began.

Dan paused. His uncle's voice told him there was something he needed to know.

"About this Granny Spenser thing. Don't be too quick to dismiss it as a lot of superstitious garbage. People believed in her. We, the family, I mean, believed in her, and believed her. There was *always* one in each generation who was considered to have 'The Sight.' Since it's obviously not been one of mine or Seth's children, we thought maybe you…"

He didn't finish his sentence.

He's hoping I can finish the sentence for him, Dan thought. *He's hoping I can tell him I have this special witchy gift, or something.* "Sorry to disappoint you, Uncle George, but I don't seem to have a special ability of this kind. So, I guess that means it's going to skip a generation here."

George could tell by the tone of his voice that Dan didn't believe him. "Actually, there could be another possibility," he responded.

"What do you mean?" asked Dan.

"Well, you know your mother came back to us after being away for several years. She came back one winter night, you in her arms, just about three months old. She only had a small paper bag of clothes with her. Of course, your grandmother and grandfather took her right back in. Dan, your mother was the one in our generation who had 'The Sight.' She never wanted to admit it, instead she made fun of it. She always got up and left the room if someone started talking about it. But you know all this, don't you?"

"Yes," Dan answered. He knew about his mother, who had run away from home, but brought her baby back—it was a boy, him—when she got sick and could not provide for herself or her baby.

Uncle George cleared his throat. "You know she was very, very ill, and died shortly after coming back to us. What you've never been told is that while she was feverish, she kept saying things like 'where's my baby?' and 'they took my baby" and 'I want my baby back.' We thought at the time, of course, that she was always referring to you, and we would bring you to her, put you in her arms. That seemed to quiet her some, but she still raved on about her baby that was gone. It was only after she passed away that we begin wondering if perhaps there was another child somewhere. We investigated. We located one place she had lived, after you were born, and one old lady in the apartment building said she sometimes saw your mother with two babies, but after several weeks, there was only one, so she thought she was just babysitting, or something. She forgot all about it. The neighbor remembered Hazel getting ill, though, and she's the one who talked her into going 'home.' And we're glad she did, of course, not only because we had you to raise, but we had our beautiful sister back with us, if only for a little while.

"She never was able to tell us why she left town so suddenly. She stayed ill until the day she died. But we loved her all we could, you know. Before and after she left."

"Yes, I know, Uncle George," Dan agreed. But what was his uncle trying to tell him now? Was he trying to say that he could have a brother or sister somewhere?

"You're telling me I could have a brother or sister, aren't you? And that this brother or sister could be the one with Granny's power. Is that it?"

Dan could almost see George shrug his shoulders on the other end of the line.

"Just a guess," he said. "But I suppose we'll never know."

"Maybe not," Dan agreed. "Let me go check this other thing out. Talk to you later, okay?"

"Sure," his uncle responded, hanging up the phone.

Dan brought his thoughts back to the problem at hand. He would worry about lost kin later.

Now, what's going on in Midland? he wondered. He certainly hadn't authorized any additional investigating of this case.

He almost made it to the door. He'd heard the phone

ringing, but whoever or whatever it was, he figured he'd let his men handle it.

"Sheriff, Sheriff, wait!" called a deputy.

The urgency in the man's voice was not lost on Dan. He turned immediately.

"What now?"

"You'll never believe this, not in a million years," his man said, very excited.

"Hey, calm down and tell me," Dan said, pushing him into a chair.

"A little girl is missing in Midland!"

Dan couldn't believe what he was hearing. "What? Say that again."

"Are you sure? Who just called? Is this a prank call, or what, with this trial? Did you get a name?"

The deputy's shoulders had sagged at the mention of a "crank call." Of course, that's probably what it was, what with the trial and all. After all, didn't they have the killer in custody?

The young man mentally chided himself. He'd worked on the force long enough not to get so excited like this.

"The name?" Dan asked.

"Oh, yeah," the man said, holding up the piece of paper in his hand. "A Marsha Miller. Says her twelve-year-old daughter, Abigail, didn't come home last night, last seen around suppertime. I asked her all the usual questions and then told her we would get to work on this right away, since it is a child. Says someone came out last evening, asked her a lot of questions and said our office would send out a bulletin right away, but I haven't seen one.

Dan gave his young deputy a look to kill.

The young man squirmed in his chair, knowing he was in trouble on this one.

"Find out who went down there," Dan said.

He simply got up, reached out, grabbed the paper from the deputy's hand, and rapidly strode to the door, telling the young man where he was headed.

He would go to Midland and take care of this himself.

Chapter 27

Colton and The Old Spenser House

Colton was back at the old house.

Too soon, he thought.

After learning from George Spencer that there was a cellar to the house, he determined to find it.

Taking one cautious step after another through the tall grass, Colton slowly made his way around to the side of the house. The side appeared to be unrevealing. Two boarded-up windows, falling eaves, but, wait—what was that? The gentle breeze of earlier had picked up and, as the tall grass swayed, Colton caught a glimpse of a frame at the foundation of the house.

"Could it be?" he wondered. "Does it really have a cellar?"

There had been no way to tell about a cellar from the front of the house.

Parting the tall grass, he revealed a small rectangular window, obviously set in the foundation at ground level for light, not entry. Debris had accumulated against the window, and it was completely dirty. But it was a window.

And a window meant a room.

Or did it?

Colton was excited but halfway fearful at the same time. None of the newspaper reports had mentioned searching a basement. On second thought, no specific areas had been mentioned, just "rooms."

What if they had missed this, somehow? What if this, or other debris, had been piled up against here, like now, and this small window had gone undetected?

Now the fears that he had experienced earlier, that he thought he had conquered, came flooding back.

The unknown was always scary.

All sorts of possibilities went through Colton's mind. He moved to go around to the back of the house to see if there was another window, or outside entrance to the cellar. Sometimes these old houses did not have full basements, just the area of one room or so dug out. As likely as not, the Spensers would have used the cellar for storing garden produce. A "root" cellar they called it. Potatoes, especially, were stored here because it was a cool, dry place and they wouldn't rot.

A single opening at the back of the house allowed a person to crawl in to store or bring out things. Shelves housed canned goods, because nearly every woman canned "back then."

Hugging as close to the shadows as possible, Colton turned the corner to the back of the house, running into even denser shrubs and thistles and what had probably been a flowerbed at one time, bordering the edge of the building.

He started parting weeds and shrubs as he nearly crawled along. Stepping down on what he thought were long-dead leaves, he sank several inches, twisting his ankle, almost causing him to lose his balance.

He knelt down, brushing away molding leaves and twigs, and found what he knew was the top of a step made of rocks put carefully in place in a row, not concrete. And these rocks had been buried in the ground for a long, long time.

Moving quickly, Colton cleared away two steps, shoved aside ivy and thistles, and discovered what he was looking for—what he had hoped was there. He found a square wooden door, still in a solid-looking frame.

Boy, they sure don't make them like they used to.

He touched the door then stopped. He had that feeling again of being watched, unseen eyes following his every movement, that at any moment someone, or something, might appear around the corner of the house, or, worse yet, pop out from behind the cellar door.

Who knows what that door might lead to or open into? Perhaps the very pit of hell, full of hideous demonic creatures ready to grab him and pull him in—punishment for having disturbed their domain.

Stop it! he chided himself. He glanced around, watching and listening for signs of danger, thinking wildly about what to do if this unseen, yet felt, evil confronted him.

Then the feeling passed. It had come and gone several times so quickly that Colton could almost believe he had never sensed anything at all, only imagined it. But his hands were clenched into tight fists and he had to force himself to relax.

The feelings had been so real that he had instinctively gone into a defensive position. He took a deep breath, scolding himself for being so ridiculous. There was nothing here to hurt him…

Just

Just don't

Just don't go

Just don't go down

Just don't go down Spenser's

Just don't go down Spenser's Lane

by yourself

EVER

Do

> *Do you*
>
> *Do you hear*
>
> *Do you hear me?*

Now why would he think of that old song?

A shiver went through him, almost a warning. But a warning of what?

He had no intention of leaving, now that he had found this old cellar door. He began inspecting it.

No one had used it in more years than Colton could guess. There was a hole at the lower left-hand corner, an entrance that some animal, or animals, had gnawed away, years ago. The sides of the hole had been worn smooth by the coming and going of many small bodies, but it was partially blocked with dirt.

No animals have used this in a long time, he decided. *But there are no small animals around here now. Has something now gone on to bigger game, such as children?*

The door was not going to open without tools. It had been boarded up very well, almost too well. These boards would have kept out King Kong, much less keep children or intruders out. But Colton wanted to check it out, anyway. Maybe check throughout the house.

But a further check of the back door proved fruitless. The house was boarded up tighter than a fortress. It certainly was going to keep people out.

Could it be keeping something in, as well?

Colton shuddered again.

Keep something in?

What something?

Would something be able to stay in and never come out? Even the smallest of creatures needed water and food.

Food.

Food? Consisting maybe of birds, mice, and other small animals that could squeeze through a small opening in a cellar door?

The thought of small animals as food for something was acceptable to Colton, but another thought came, completely unbidden.

What about children as food? something asked from within himself, a thought from a level of his mind he did not know existed.

Colton's nerves began to tingle and his stomach churned.

Cannibalism? Could it be? What a thought.

Someone who only developed the craving for human meat every three years and found out, after the first one, that eleven-year-old children tasted good?

Colton took several deep breaths, trying to compose himself after such a horrid thought.

It must be this place. A person never quite forgets his childhood fears and this house was the center of fears for many children, past and present.

He had been foolish to come here alone. If whatever

had taken the children was here, it had tasted human blood and flesh. It might, just might, decide to come after him.

Colton stood still and, as the minutes ticked by, he kept getting the feeling more and more that something wasn't quite right about this place.

The same feeling as before.

He was becoming increasingly edgy and nervous. Still, he continued to the back door, his heart pounding. Although it was boarded up, Colton was able to see through the slats. He could see a small area, of what probably was the kitchen, and a door.

A patch of faded, brittle wallpaper was beginning to peel away from the wall, hanging down.

And what was that? It looked like a doorframe, the crack of a door.

But if it were a door, it had been boarded up and covered over, somehow made smooth and wallpaper put up over it. No one could tell a door was even there.

It fit! What had Spenser said? His old grandmother had insisted the evil came from the cellar and had argued until they had closed it up.

Obviously, no one had bothered to ask the Spenser boys any questions about the house during the investigations. Surely, if they had, they would have looked for and found this sealed up basement door.

Had the previous search parties missed this and the small basement window, barely visible above ground, in all the debris and ivy? Yes, it would have been entirely possible to miss the small side window of the cellar and the door had been completely covered by thick, dry ivy and weeds.

The Spensers had moved away at least ten years before the girls started disappearing, so it was possible things were overgrown long before then. And who could predict wallpaper? It may have only recently given way at that spot, revealing the door crack and frame.

It could only be the door to the cellar, a door leading down. Didn't George Spenser say Granny had made them close up the cellar?

Colton moved around, standing on his toes, hoping to get a better view through the boards.

A beam of light from a hole in the roof streamed across the dusty floor, in front of the concealed door, and glistened off an object on the floor.

Colton wanted to see what the object was.

With a strength he didn't know he possessed, he started pulling on the boards nailed across the back door. He looked around the old porch and spied a stray board. Using it as a lever, he worked until he removed the middle boards, allowing just enough room for his body to crawl through the crack.

He hammered at the board that had been placed over what was once glass in the door until it gave way.

Colton straightened up, catching his breath. He had not stopped until the task of breaking in had been completed. He let the board he had used as a level and battering ram fall from his hand, where it hit the old boards of the porch with a loud clatter.

He jumped, startled. He was covered with sweat, even had it dripping off his forehead. Wiping it off with a sleeve, he took a deep breath, willing himself to become still and calm. He had been making enough noise that, had anyone been here, they could certainly have slipped up on him as he worked.

Now, many thoughts assaulted him as he realized the foolishness of his deed. If someone were in the old house, might he be waiting to jump Colton? And Colton had just let him out—had given him…it?…a way to the outside world.

Colton felt he was on to something important, though, so he bent to step through the opening he had made. As he rose up on the other side, a multitude of odors rushed at him. He almost gagged. Dust, mustiness, decay, were his first thoughts, yet under that was something else—something like a dead animal, but different, sweeter smelling, maybe. He couldn't quite put his finger on it.

He had no desire to stay a second longer than necessary in this creepy old place, so he crossed the space to the object in three long strides, bending to pick it up.

Letting the object fall into the middle of his hand, Colton was about to laugh at himself and toss the object away when something stopped him.

He closed his fist around the object, almost involuntarily.

ʚ໒ʚ໒

"No" he cried, reaching for the wall to support himself. He almost fell down.

Not here, not here, at least let me get away from here!

But he couldn't stop the fugue which brought the pictures, just as he had never been able to before.

The little girl was talking to him, and this time he could hear her.

"Please, Colton, please walk with me to ball practice. You don't have to talk to me, just let me walk with you! Please!"

The pleading was unmistakable in her voice. The voice had come this time before the picture, and somehow he knew he was about to see the identity of the little girl. And, yes, it was because of this place, the fact that he was here.

The picture became clear, and Colton was looking into the face of Little Annie Mercer, her expression eager with the thought of walking to ball practice with him. They were standing at a corner where they had met, coming from different directions.

And now another part of the picture came clear to him. Little Annie reached up and removed her ball cap.

Colton saw a blue barrette holding back her hair on each side of her forehead.

Little Annie wore barrettes? Little Annie, the tomboy?

The picture faded as quickly as it had come, leaving Colton trembling, breathing hard. He started to shiver. This was the most powerful vision yet.

So real!

He wanted away from here. He knew he would come back to see what was behind the door in the middle of the house, but he wanted some equipment with him.

He was out the opening, around the house, and back to The Lane before he realized he was there.

He continued rapidly down The Lane, almost running back to his car. He did not look back, wanting to forget what he had just learned there.

☙❧☙

It quivered all over. It sensed the human, sensed food, long before the human reached the bend of The Lane as he stood before the house.

It forced itself to be very still, hardly breathing. It was not hungry, not having finished its last catch yet, and just recently having captured new prey. This new prey that was still alive, but in what would shortly be an endless sleep.

If the thing could have had a concept of "luck," it

would have considered itself lucky. Just as it was about to finish this last food, another food source had come within its range. And, although it would normally have finished its last food and even rested a long while before searching for more, the urge to collect more had been so strong it could not contain it.

Unlike before, it had no need to capture its food this time. The prey was already lying on the ground. When it discovered the prey was still breathing, it was so excited it could hardly pick it up and carry it to its lair.

But it had.

⌘

By the time Colton spotted the end of The Lane where it connected with Elm Street, he was half jogging, half stumbling along.

He remembered what he had read in the newspaper articles, but he wanted to be sure, be positive of his facts before he acted upon what he knew, instinctively, was true.

Something was in the cellar of the old Spenser House. He had felt its presence, that was the feeling he had several times there.

So close to it!

Something sinister and horrible was hiding there, eating all the small animals around and luring bigger prey only once every three years or so. Colton was convinced of it. Had it been only two years this time? And had it been Abigail?

He reached his car and opened the door automatically, his mind racing. He shuddered to think that children could be considered prey, yet everything seemed to be pointing that way.

Human beings, in their arrogance and pride in being at what they considered the top of the food chain, could not and would not think of themselves as food for anything else.

Oh, sure, there was the occasional attack on man by a wild beast in some part of the world, but the beast was usually driven to attack by unusual, unnatural circumstances. The depletion of a natural prey and hunger were usually the reasons. And such renegades were quickly disposed of.

But what if humans were faced with a predator that deliberately and carefully stalked and drew them to it as a natural order of life?

Could such a species have evolved from any known animal? Or did it arrive on earth from somewhere else.

Colton knew several people, including some on his police force, who believed in UFOs and intelligent life on other planets, but he had never been persuaded. He always listened politely, made the right comments, but never was convinced. Maybe he was one of the many who thought the human race the one and only superior species.

He opened his hand and stared at the small object there. It was a blue barrette, the same blue barrette in his vision, holding back Little Annie's hair.

Nineteen plus years ago, it probably had been too dark next to the baseboard to be seen when the search parties had looked through the boards and into the old house. Nineteen plus years ago, that small hole in the roof, allowing the sunlight to shine off the barrette, had not been a hole at all, the roof probably still being intact in that spot.

How it was so easily missed.

He put his hands up and gripped the steering wheel, his head on his arms.

"Oh, Little Annie," he cried, "if I had only let you walk to ball practice with me, you would never have disappeared! Please, please forgive me! I was so worried about being teased by the other guys. I didn't want to be seen with any girl. It wasn't just you, Annie. It wasn't just you Please forgive me."

He realized he was gripping the blue barrette so tightly he thought he would break it. He slowly opened his hand and leaned back in his seat, his eyes still wet with tears. The blue barrette stared up at him in silent accusation. He felt drained, as if someone had kicked the wind out of him. He had always been strong. Never had he hesitated in many split-second decisions on a case or in the field. He had saved many lives by moving quickly and without hesitation.

Only once, had a perp surprised him, and that was because he himself had surprised the man in the act of robbing a convenience store. Colton was off duty at the time but responded instinctively by drawing his revolver. The perp also responded rapidly by kicking the gun out of Colton's hand and punching him in the gut as the gun flew away. A major fistfight had followed, which tore up many shelves and displays in the store. Colton had returned punch for punch until backup arrived. The perp had been so involved in beating him, so angry at being interrupted, that he did not hear the backup until too late.

He was taken into custody and Colton was taken to the emergency room. He had several cracked ribs and more cuts and bruises than he cared to remember. He had spent the night in the hospital being "observed," then spent the next couple of days around the office, moving very slowly and carefully.

Colton felt right now, as if he had been beaten up far worse than that. He couldn't do anything for Little Annie now. He refused to take the blame for that day nineteen years ago. He felt it wasn't revealed to him to make him feel guilty after all this time but to provide clues for him to find and kill the kidnapper.

The time was right.

He knew what he was going to do now and what he needed to do it with.

Chapter 28

Abigail

Abigail could think, but she could not move. She felt just like she did at the dentist's office. She had such sensitive teeth that the dentist always had to sedate her before she could stand to let him give her a shot in her gums.

With the sedation dentistry, she completely relaxed, clear down to her eyelids, and they always involuntarily closed on her. Her hands, which she would clasp together on her lap when she first sat down in the dentist's chair, came apart of their own volition and fell to her sides. She had that same feeling now.

She would like to be able to open her eyes, to see where she was, but she just couldn't move.

Unfortunately, she could still smell very well. She identified dust, a musty, old odor, and then something else that she could not identify. The odor was almost like when they were driving along on the highway, and they could smell a dead animal somewhere, maybe not a skunk, but something.

On those occasions, however, the odor fainted away as they traveled on. But here she could not get away from it. It had a nauseating, suffocating quality about it. She wanted to gag, but couldn't. Nor could she get away from the odors.

The last thing she remembered was pedaling her bike very fast down Elm Street. Then, she suddenly hit something on the street large enough to make her bike flip up and over. She hit her head on a large rock as she hit the ground.

Then she woke up in this place. At least her mind did.

It felt creepy.

Mama! she cried, silently, suddenly filled with an unprecedented fear. This was a fear so complete and foreign to her that she didn't think she could bear it.

It was worse than coming across a snake in the yard, or having a spider crawl on her. She had always had an obsessive fear of spiders.

She screamed silently as she felt something touch her left leg and begin a slow ascent upward. It was cold to the touch, although she was already cold in this room. It only lasted a few seconds, however, and was withdrawn when she heard a sound overhead and to her left.

Someone was rescuing her! She knew her mom would come!

Help! she cried, but only in her mind, since no muscles responded or moved to her brain's command to speak. *Help! Help me!*

She associated the sounds with someone moving around boards, which held no reference for her. She had no idea where she was. She had no idea she was in the cellar of the old Spenser House.

Since she had heard all the stories about the place, if she had known she was there, her fear would probably have caused her heart to stop.

Help, oh, please, help me! Please! she cried, silently, willing herself to move.

When the sounds stopped and all was quiet again, she felt such dread, a complete hopelessness. She prayed that someone, especially her mother, would find her soon. She also prayed that the thing, which had touched her leg earlier, would not return. The thought of spiders or tarantulas crawling on her caused her such anxiety she felt her heart pounding wildly.

She had no idea that her fears were sensed by something across the room from her, something that lived on and grew more powerful by her fear.

Although she could see nothing, and the place was unusually quiet, she had the feeling that someone…something?…was out there, not far away.

Something that was watching, and waiting.

Chapter 29

Back at the Old Spenser House

It quivered all over, rippling from the center out to the tip of its fingers. It had just reached out to touch the food across the room, but withdrew quickly when it felt the human coming. Actually, it *sensed* the human above it.

This wasn't its prey.

It was too large.

Part of the joy of capturing its prey was the delight it took in the fear it caused the helpless creatures. The last sudden rush of fluids was unnamed to it, but was very exciting to it, the first excitement for it, the last sensation for its prey.

So it had kept this latest prey alive.

It had been pure luck that it happened upon this prey. It had been on the ground, seemingly just waiting to be picked up and carried back here.

But the one that it had sensed above was different. Had he felt the presence of this one before? A few had responded over the time of its existence in this strange place, but many more had not. At least, it thought the prey had always come to him because he willed it to.

Now, as before, when one of these creatures did not respond, it knew it just had to be still and the creature would go away, not be a threat to it. With its innate instinct for survival, it became so still it would not have been detected with even the most sophisticated sensors. It could have been dead—its metabolism and life signs slowed so much.

When it felt the human enter its protective structure and move around above it, it stayed motionless. Then it stayed motionless a long time after the noise above it stopped.

And only when the presence above it had been gone a long time did it slowly begin to breathe again.

It eyed the prey, still alive, that it had captured recently.

Soon…soon…

Chapter 30

Colton and Marsha

First, Colton wanted to stop by and pick up Marsha. He was going to have to drive to Fort Smith, for certain items, and he simply wanted her company. He liked her with him as much as possible. He wasn't going to lose her now, after all these years.

He spotted her in the swing as soon as he started up the sidewalk. A few long strides brought him up the steps and to her.

She didn't even have time to stand up before he grabbed her hands.

"Come on, come with me to Fort Smith," he said, urging her to come with him down the steps.

"Fort Smith!" she exclaimed, hesitating and drawing back a little. "Why?"

"Please!"

"But what if they find Abigail or she returns and I'm not here? I need to be here!"

"She won't be coming back, not unless we help and not unless we hurry."

"What do you mean? What did you find out at the old Spenser House?"

"I'll tell you on the way. Now, come on. Please."

Marsha allowed Colton to coax her along but she was apprehensive about the whole situation. But she realized that Colton was very excited about something and she knew she would trust him with her life.

They were in the car and going through the streets of Midland before she had time to start asking questions. She waited until they turned north on the highway toward Fort Smith before she turned toward him. "Okay, now, what did you find? Something about Abigail?"

Glancing over at her, he saw the anticipation in her face. He could only hope what he suspected about the old Spenser House was true.

"Not exactly," he began, "but I know I found out more than all the previous search parties sent to find the other girls."

He held out his right hand, still closed around the blue barrette, knuckles up. She automatically held out her open palm, as most people did when someone wants to give them something. Colton opened his fist and the blue barrette fell into her palm.

She wasn't sure what she had been expecting, but it certainly wasn't this dirty thing. "What's this?" she asked, "A barrette? Abigail doesn't even wear barrettes. Her hair is short and curly. Is this the big discovery?"

"Marsha, it's a *blue* barrette, a very old blue barrette. Don't you remember what we read in the newspaper articles about the little girls? Little Annie had a blue barrette in her hair the day she disappeared."

Marsha thought that perhaps he had gone completely mad. Maybe there was something unnatural about The Old Spenser House and it had affected his senses. "But Little Annie was the first girl to disappear! Don't you remember her? How many years ago is that now?"

She stopped, trying to figure out exactly when it had been. She had not really paid much attention to the dates on the old newspapers. She just remembered people talking about it at the time. But she would not have remembered that if Abigail had not disappeared and Colton appeared. He seemed so caught up in something, but nothing that made any sense to her.

"Nineteen-fifty-seven, that's when. Almost twenty years ago now, that's how long," he supplied.

"But how could you find this after almost twenty years? Why didn't others find it? And, besides, how do you know it's Little Annie's? There are lots of blue barrettes and probably lots of kids that have explored around

The Old Spenser House. It could have belonged to any-one."

But even as she said that, she knew that just wasn't so. Even as children, they did not go near the place. No one ever did. There was just something about it. Too spooky.

"...not like this," he was saying. "Look at it, at the little grooves and curls."

She held it closer to her face, carefully examining it. It was plastic, shaped like a bow and in the grooves of the bow there was dirt—embedded dirt. She turned it over. The backside was filthy. "This doesn't prove anything," she protested. "It wouldn't take a barrette long to get dirty."

"There are some things I haven't told you," he said, quietly.

Marsha looked over at him. His voice had a funny catch in it.

"Oh?" she asked.

For the next several miles, he told her about the "pictures" that came to him, visions that he had been seeing off and on for the last year.

"You see," he concluded. "I never once could see her face until this last time as I stood in the old Spenser House, holding this blue barrette. I actually felt as if Granny Spenser was standing there, watching me, putting thoughts and ideas into my mind. I know this belonged to Little Annie, I know she lost it right there, in that old house, and I *know* there's something in the cellar. Now, where's the nearest army supply store?" he asked, without giving her a chance to respond to his last comment.

They had arrived at the southern edge of Fort Smith, and he needed to know which way to go, whether to get on the by-pass and exit somewhere or continue on Towson Avenue to downtown.

The only army surplus store she could think of was on Garrison Avenue, in the old downtown part of Fort Smith. Unfortunately, there was no quick and easy way to get there, except to continue in the heavy traffic on Towson. After all, it was Saturday, a traditional shopping day for a lot of people.

It was also the first of the month and that brought out a lot of senior citizens to shop, who had just received their social security checks.

Colton usually avoided shopping at this time of the month, but there was no choice now. But it did make the traffic more congested, and he cursed several times on the lack of progress in several places.

Marsha kept quiet, knowing she could say nothing to help while he concentrated on the traffic and driving. She just hoped he wasn't stopped and given a ticket, the way he was weaving in and out of lanes, trying to get to where he was going faster.

She was almost convinced by his tone that he knew what he was doing, and he was certainly in a hurry. But then doubts set in.

Did she really know this man? Twelve years was a long time. Maybe he had changed so much from the young man of eighteen she left behind that she wouldn't like him, much less love him, now. No, her heart wouldn't let her think he had changed at all, at least not in the ways that counted.

She was going to sit in the car when they pulled in front of the army surplus store. This store was in an old building, one of the many old storefronts that had been abandoned by retail clothing stores. Those stores had long since moved out to the east side of town, either into the new Central Mall or out close to it. The owners knew that's where all the trade would be in the future.

That left the older, downtown part of Fort Smith with many empty buildings. On one side of the army surplus there was a used bookstore. *Trade Two for One* was painted on the window. There was an empty space on the other side, then an old hardware store.

"Will you come in with me? I need you to help me carry some things," he asked, when he noticed she wasn't moving.

She smiled. "Oh, is that why you brought me along, to carry things for you?"

He was relieved to see she still had her sense of humor, in spite of the situation and the things he had just asked her to believe. "No, of course not, you know better than that!"

He smiled in return as he got out and went around

the car to help her out. They walked into the store hand in hand. He quickly located the first of the items he was after. Although he noticed her quizzical looks, he did not explain why he was choosing the items he was.

She silently received and held the things for him as he moved around the store. Some things were too heavy or awkward for her, so he carried them.

They were looking at things in the center aisle of the store, her opposite him, when she felt him right next to her.

"Don't look toward the front window right now," he whispered in her ear, "but there's that little old lady in the black dress again, the one I told you about, looking in here and nodding at me. Again!"

"You're kidding." She grinned. "Has she changed her hat yet?"

"I'm serious," he said, firmly. "Now, look!"

She turned to look, seeing no one.

"She's sure spry for her age," Marsha said, shaking her head.

Colton looked up quickly. Seeing the old lady gone, he pushed the box he was carrying into Marsha's arms and raced to the front door, throwing it open. There was no one on the sidewalk for several stores in either direction.

She had to have gone into one of the other stores. Scanning the few cars parked in front, Colton motioned for Marsha to put the purchases on the checkout counter and come to the door, which she did, telling the clerk they'd be right back.

Colton had Marsha search one store while he looked through another.

They met out front again, neither having spotted the old lady.

"But, there was a back door to the bookstore," Marsha said, pointing to the one she had checked.

"Maybe she went out that way. It is that important to find her?"

"It must not be," Colton responded, "or we would, don't you think?"

"You're asking me—*moi*—what I think about all this?"

Colton simply gave her a hard look.

They paid for their purchases, and it did take both of them, making several trips, to carry them to the car.

As they pulled away from the store, her curiosity finally got the best of her, although she had promised herself not to say a word.

"Are you going to tell me what your plan is?"

"Not now," he answered. "I'm going on all my instincts, all my feelings. If I happen to be wrong, which is always a possibility, then I'm going to feel foolish enough." He paused. "But I *know* I'm not wrong."

Marsha couldn't decide to believe if he were right or wrong. At least he thought he was right. She had nothing in reply and they traveled in silence back down Towson

Avenue, south toward Midland. They were both lost in their own thoughts.

His, reviewing all the things he had bought, hoping he had covered everything.

Marsha's thoughts returned to her daughter. Whatever he was planning, she hoped and prayed it would work.

She was the first to break the silence as they headed out of town. "Whatever you're going to do, don't you think you should call the county sheriff's office and let them help you?"

"No, there's no time," he said. "And, besides, why should they believe me? My theory is based on Granny Spenser, Old Man Ogden, a hidden cellar, visions of old ladies, and an old, dirty blue barrette. I mean, what's wrong with this picture? Right?"

He looked over at her. "So, who in their right mind is going to believe me? Huh?"

She didn't know if he really expected an answer or not. "Well, actually, all that's all right, you know," she said drily. "For a minute there, I thought you were only basing your ideas on the facts we found."

Her sarcasm was not lost on him.

"Marsha," he began.

But she held up her hand, stopping him. "Sorry, it really is okay. But you've never mentioned anything to me about Old Man Ogden. And don't say a word because, at this point, I really don't think I want to know. Just do your thing."

They rode on in silence for a few minutes.

"She was crazy, you know," she said.

"Who was crazy? What are you talking about?" he asked, looking over at her.

"Granny Spenser. I heard all my life that she was crazy, imagined things. I especially remember my grandmother talking about her. Granny was still alive and lived there when my grandmother was a little girl.

"I heard she had psychic powers, saw visions of things that came true, told people things that had happened, then everyone found out they had."

"Didn't you grow up in the same Midland I did?" she asked. "Didn't you hear the same stores?"

"Yes, of course, I did," he answered. "But I also talked to one of her grandsons on the phone this morning and found out a lot more things, from someone who really knew her, then all the stories went together."

"I'm lost," Marsha said. "You've confused me completely. Are you still looking for Abigail, or what?"

"Of course, I am," he replied. "That's why I'm breaking the speed limit right now getting back to Midland."

"Well, I know this sounds like a very stupid question, since you obviously know more of what's going on than I do, but what does Granny Spenser have to do with finding Abigail? Did everyone only think she died years ago, and did you run into her at that old house today, or something?"

He heard the teasing in her voice, but he was serious. "Maybe I did," he said, quietly.

Marsha was silent. She was trying to think of something to say, to respond, when he spoke again.

"The old lady in the black dress that I've seen several times…well…that's Granny Spenser," he said, knowing how it sounded and knowing she would not believe him. Hell, he wouldn't have believed it, either. Or at least not yesterday.

"Oh. And how do you know that?" *I had to ask,* she thought. *I just had to ask, didn't I?*

"Actually, Old Man Ogden told me. He knew her personally."

"Ah, I was beginning to wonder where and how Old Man Ogden came into all this."

"Look, I know how all this sounds. I know you don't believe any of it, but at least trust me, okay? Please?"

He reached for her hand and for a fleeting second she almost pulled hers away. But because he was who he was, she allowed him to touch her. They rode along, her hand in his. She felt very secure like this, just not sure of what she was hearing.

"But I saw her, too," exclaimed Marsha. "She wasn't a vision, or dead. She was real."

"Exactly," Colton said.

Exactly? Now, what does he mean by that? "Exactly?" she asked. "Something can't be a vision and be real, both at the same time."

"Are you sure?" he asked.

"Would you stop it?" she asked, exasperated. "Can't you give me a straight answer here, not just questions with questions?"

"You asked me, I told you. If she's real, where does she disappear to? Thin air, it seems. So you saw her. Where did she go? I wasn't two seconds behind her, you immediately after me."

Marsha shrugged. "Maybe she went into one of the other shops, into the bathroom or office, or something. I don't know. Just because she wasn't visible, doesn't mean she wasn't there."

"Exactly," he said, again, agreeing with her.

"Not again, please. You've thoroughly confused me here. There are no such things as ghosts, or people living in some sort of parallel universe with our own. What we see is what we get."

"Do you really think so?"

"Will you please stop answering with questions?"

"Sure, but I just want you to stop and think about some things here. Just because we were taught one thing, always believed it, doesn't mean there aren't other beliefs and realities out there. What about extra-terrestrial beings? Life forms from other planets? Do you believe there could be?"

She pulled her hand away, leaning back in the corner of her seat, against the door, and just stared at him.

"Well, do you?" he asked, again.

"I don't think so," she replied.

"Why not?" he asked.

She saw he was serious. He really was serious. *Okay.* She decided to play along. "I don't know, really. Do you?"

"I think so."

"You *think* so? Don't you know for sure if you do or don't?" she asked. "Why ask me such a question if you're not sure yourself?"

"Can't I ask you what you believe without knowing what I believe myself?"

"No," she said, very firmly. She wasn't going to let him off the hook that easily.

He smiled at her.

"Now you sound like a woman," he said, grinning.

"I am a woman," she replied, turning her head and looking out the window.

"I know," he said, quietly, and in such a way it made her turn back to look at him.

He was looking at her with such a lecherous expression on his face that she had to laugh.

"So, what do you believe about them?" she asked. "*Is* there life on other planets?"

"Could be," he said, "and why not? Why should we assume that this planet is the only one inhabited? If there were an explosion in space, why was this planet the only one to have formed? I believe there could easily be other planets, far beyond our universe and beyond our knowledge. The inhabitants of those planets could also easily be far more advanced than we are at this point, with technology capable of allowing them to travel from planet to planet, just as we travel from state to state in cars or country to country in airplanes.

"And, these 'people,' if we want to call them that, may not *be* that. Their species may feed on humans or anything else, or things we've never even heard or dreamed of."

"Can you tell me why this may not be possible? Can you?"

Marsha was again silent. She was beginning to feel sort of foolish. It seemed she never had an answer ready, or was even capable of thinking. Of course, it had been a terrible eighteen hours. She had not slept since yesterday, early evening, so she felt she had a right to not be able to think, or even want to think, especially when the questions were so unexpected.

"Well, I do suppose it *could* be possible. But have you ever seen a UFO, or anything?" she asked.

"No, not personally, just talked with several who thought they had, and—"

"That's just it," Marsha interrupted.

He looked at her as if she were crazy. "What's just it? What are you talking about?"

"You said you had talked to several who *thought* they had seen UFOs. *Thought*, Colton, just thought? Don't they really know? Or did some psychiatrist somewhere convince them they had seen it, maybe in order to write a book, or for some other personal gain?"

"What I was going to say before you interrupted me," he began, looking over at her, "was that I never really believed in them, or that there could even conceivably be life on other planets until this thing—this thing right now. I'm a part of this, so that makes it believable."

"Just because you think something is true, is that supposed to make it believable to others?"

"Well, there are other things," Colton admitted, again.

"Other things? What now?" she asked.

"There are also the visions I've been having," he replied.

"Visions? Like in dreams?" she asked.

"No, not dreams. I'm always awake with these. I know I am."

"Or you dream you are," she responded.

Colton grinned over at her. "You have an answer for everything, don't you?" He shrugged. "Could be, I suppose, sometimes, at least. But most of the time I am definitely awake."

He paused. They listened to the hum of the tires on the pavement as they sped along. The fan on the thermostat-controlled air conditioner clicked on, increasing the hum but cooling the car even more.

She still felt warm. "I'll bite. So what do you see in these visions?" she asked.

"For the past year I've seen a little girl, talking to someone else I can't see. The little girl is looking at me, but I've never been able to see her face, just a blank where her face should be. I've seen the back of someone's head facing away from me. I've had the feeling each time I should know who it is and what they're trying to tell me. But it just left me at that point. Until today," he added.

"Until today?" she repeated. "So, what happened today?"

"This morning, before you came to the newspaper office, I had the vision as I was reading about the missing girls. The figure turned toward me, walked toward me, as if I were a camera. He came closer, and yes, it was a he. In fact, it was me!"

"You?"

"Yes, me as a boy. Around twelve, I would guess. I knew it was me even before I recognized the boy in my own photos. My mom keeps a photo of me at that age on her hall table. "It was me all right."

"And the little girl?" she asked.

"Still faceless. That was the bad part. The vision left me with such a feeling of emptiness, a void, and something else, too."

Marsha looked over at him as he paused, expecting him to continue. He seemed to be lost in his own world suddenly.

"Something else?" she urged.

"Oh, yeah," He shook his head, as if bringing his thoughts back to the present. "Fear, apprehension, I think. It was almost like I didn't want to know the rest of the vision, like whatever was left to be revealed, I didn't really want to know, to face."

"Death?" she suggested.

"No, just something there I didn't want to face. And, then, just before I picked the barrette up, while I was at the old Spenser House, after I found it, the vision struck again. This time, I saw the face of the little girl, and I had been right. I didn't want to know what it revealed to me."

Marsha remained quiet, knowing he would tell the story in his own way, in his own time. This part of him had not changed. He couldn't be rushed.

"You see," he continued. "It was Little Annie."

"Little Annie?" she repeated. "As in Little Annie who disappeared?"

He nodded.

"Did she tell you what happened to her, by any chance? Where she is now?"

She could barely keep the sarcasm, the unbelief, out of her voice.

He shot her a warning glance, which was not lost on her.

"Sorry," she said. "But you'll have to admit you're asking me to believe a lot here."

"Yes, I know. I just have to ask you to believe me, and trust me. And I do know that's quite a lot to swallow at this point."

She nodded, catching a sob in her throat.

He reached over and patted her hands, which were folded on her lap in front of her.

"Well, if she didn't tell you what happened, what did she say to you?"

"She was talking to me as a boy. She was asking, begging really, for me to walk with her to ball practice."

"So?" Marsha hadn't made the connection yet. It wasn't her vision.

"Don't you see? We happened to meet on the way to ball practice the day she disappeared. When we met, she asked me to walk with her the rest of the way to practice. Being a typical boy, I refused and turned away from her.

"And?"

"Don't you see?" he repeated. "If I had let her walk with me to ball practice, she wouldn't have disappeared, wouldn't have been kidnapped. I would have been there with her. It's my fault she was kidnapped," he ended, his voice full of self-accusation and guilt.

"Bull!" she said, loudly, actually causing him to swerve. That was the last reaction he had expected from her.

"You don't believe I had this vision?" he asked.

"Oh, I believe you could have had a vision, or even many visions in the past year. What I don't believe, and will not accept, is the self-guilt you're carrying all of a sudden because you think it's your fault that Little Annie disappeared. And all because of a vision. A dream! What is a dream, anyway, and why do people have them? I mean, maybe you ate something each time that disagreed with you, or you had a lot of stress at work at that particular time. There are many factors that cause people to dream. I used to have nightmares if I ate pizza too late, right before I went to bed."

Colton gave her a look that showed her exactly what he thought of her comments. She could tell what he was thinking. Eating pizza had nothing to do with these visions of his. They were more real, more vivid than any physical or emotionally-induced dream or nightmare.

"I should have walked with her," he said.

"That's not true," she disagreed. "As a boy, you had no idea of what was coming. And boys always scorn and turn away from girls of that age. It's a tradition, I think. Or at least an age requirement."

He couldn't be sure if she were serious or not.

"Really," she said. "I taught sixth graders before I moved back here. I saw it on the school ground all the time, during recess period. And girls that age continue to set themselves up for it. We need to get away from these preset roles you see developing at an early age. But that's a discussion for another time, of course. You're simply not to blame. Who knows? You might have been kidnapped, also."

He hadn't thought of that. "What about this?" he asked, returning to their previous subject. "If you want to believe in only one god—God—then there's even a place in the Bible that says that the sons of God came down to earth, married human women, and produced a race of giants. If these 'people' were sons of God, wouldn't they have superior intellect, superior everything to humans, who are merely creations of God? And, if these sons of God were willing and able to come to earth and dwell here—although we really don't know if they stayed or not—they might just have come down for a bit of fun."

Marsha managed to look shocked at this.

Colton grinned and then continued, "If they came down, why could there not be other life forms that are able and willing to come to earth? Other creations, even, of the same God? If so, could they not have superior or at least equal intelligence to humans? And what if they had other orientations, that is, other brain patterns, thoughts, so that other things could be food for them, other creations we can't even imagine, perhaps. Why couldn't there be such creatures existing somewhere?"

Marsha really had never thought about it.

"Who do you think the 'sons of God' were?" Colton asked.

Marsha just shook her head. She didn't know. "I can't think about that when all I can think about is Abigail! Thinking about what may be happening to her is…is…unthinkable, really. You're a policeman. Tell me truthfully. Just how many, what percentage, of girls, young ladies, older women even, are found alive after being kidnapped? How many, Colton?"

She caught a sob in her throat, doing her best not to let the tears fall, although they were forming. She started fumbling in her purse for a handkerchief.

"Glove box," he said, simply, pointing to the dash.

She opened the glove box and brought out a small, compact package of tissues.

He didn't want to answer her question. Actually, he hadn't even allowed himself to think about the situation, except in a positive way, that Abigail was still alive and he would find her in time. In time before what? He knew that's what Marsha was asking. And she was right. Only a small, a very small, percentage of girls, ladies, were found or came out of a kidnapping situation unscathed, untouched in some way. Those few who were untouched physically still had emotional and mental problems with it later. The usual situation was rape, at the very least. But the most common was rape and mutilation, then death. Bodies were found in various stages of mutilations, the product of some psycho who tortured and maimed by cutting circles around breasts and genitalia, to beatings with weird objects. In any case, rape was usually present. For the very few who survived the tortures while captive, they never mentally recovered.

A recent situation from near his home came to mind. In this case, a thirty-year-old mother of two disappeared. A few months later, a truck driver picked her up wandering down the interstate highway, naked and in a daze. She knew who she was, but told stories of torture, various items being inserted into her vagina, continual rapes. Her family tried to love her, she took therapy, but after about a year, she committed suicide, leaving a note saying she just could not cope anymore. Death was a release from what she had suffered at the hands of a psycho. Family members of those who were kidnapped had a hard time coping, also. Just thinking about your loved one being tortured, the physical pain alone being unbearable, sent many family members into such emotional states they never recovered. Families and friends never seemed to know how to treat those who returned, turning situations awkward.

Life was never the same.

When someone presumed to have the right to interrupt another person's life by kidnapping and doing whatever they wanted to that person, in his or her deranged state, a precious soul was lost. That these types could do that to another life had always been beyond Colton's reasoning.

He had been hoping, by discussing other things, to help keep her mind off Abigail and the possible consequences of a kidnapping. No, Colton had, not and would not, allow himself to think of those things in connection with Abigail. He wanted to be her hero, rescuing her just in time, untying her from the railroad track, and pulling her off just before the train arrived, just like in the old serial films he had watched as a kid.

He refused to let reality set in. Only by picturing her

alive did he have the strength to go on. Marsha could break down and cry, but he had to remain strong, for both of them.

He told her she should go home and convinced her by saying she needed to be there now in case they did hear something about Abigail.

She had a confused, questioning look on her face. "Didn't you intend for me to go with you?" she asked.

"Never. Why would you think such a thing? It's much too dangerous."

"Then why did you—"

"Shh!" he interrupted, putting his fingers to her mouth.

She took them away.

"But—the equipment—"

"I'll manage. I'm a big, strong boy now. Please. Go home, okay? Just for me?"

She acquiesced but still had a puzzled look on her face. It had been obvious to her that she was going to help. She wondered why he had changed his mind but knew he wasn't going to explain further.

Secretly, she was glad to be going home. In case he was wrong, she should be home.

Neither wanted to think about his being wrong.

Chapter 30

Colton and Dan

Colton kept his hands in sight as the officer climbed out of the patrol car. One hand he put on top of the car, the other he put on top of the open driver's door. He knew, as a cop himself that they wanted to be able to see both hands of the person they were approaching, so they would not get nervous and wonder where those hands were or what they were doing. If the officer could not see hands, they thought of all sorts of possibilities.

More than one state patrolman or city policeman had been shot, even killed, by weapons in the hands of perps or people they had stopped. Those were hands they had carelessly forgotten to check for until it was too late, until they were too close to defend themselves.

So, Colton kept his hands still and firmly in place.

The other man kept his eye on Colton as he rounded the front of his vehicle, then the officer came to a sudden stop.

Colton stood up taller, unable to believe what he was seeing.

Neither man moved, only stared at the other. The deputy took off his sunglasses, but that only confirmed a fact that both men had instantly realized.

"Well." Colton smiled. "I've always heard that everyone has a twin in this world somewhere. Now I believe it."

Dan said nothing, still staring at Colton. After having just heard that he may or may not have had a brother or sister somewhere, it had never occurred to him that perhaps that person was a brother and the brother was a twin. Looking at the man standing in front of him was just one more thing added to this day to shatter his world of reality.

Why was his world coming apart? Why was his ordered, organized, never-changing world changing so rapidly? Would this day of surprises never end?

"We not only could pass as twins," Colton said, nodding toward Dan's patrol car, "but we're also in the same line of business."

"You a cop?" Dan asked.

"Yeah," Colton answered. "Work out of the city, near Chicago. Don't tell me you went into this business for the same reason I did."

"And why was that?" Dan asked, interested in spite of himself.

Neither man had moved any closer to the other. They were still sizing each other up, wondering just what to believe.

Yes, why was that? Colton wondered, *What had been the difference in this job and countless others?* "I figured there would be a lot of action, lots of territory to cover, people to meet, things to see and do, more to experience. So what's your reason?"

Dan shrugged. "Some of the same, I reckon. So what are you doing here? You've covered quite a lot of territory right now, today, from Chicago to Midland."

Colton wasn't ready to tell his real reason for being here. He wasn't yet sure whether this man would be with him or against him. He couldn't take the chance on anything holding him up right now. "The scenery," he replied, without hesitation. "Definitely the scenery. Just smell that freshly mowed hay."

Colton took a deep breath. He was hoping this man was on a routine trip through his assigned area and would soon leave.

"Don't BS me," the other man said. "I got a call about a stranger in town, a little girl missing, and the mother of the missing girl driving off with a stranger.

You're the stranger, complete with Illinois tags. So, what are you doing here?" he repeated.

"You won't believe it," Colton began, spreading his hands. "You really won't, and I really don't have time to tell you. But—" He hesitated then decided to take a chance on this man. "Will you trust me, let me take care of some things I need to? Then I'll come and explain everything to you. Scout's honor."

Colton held up his fingers in the Boy Scout sign. He knew the other man wouldn't fall for it as soon as he said it but stranger things had happened. *Yeah*, he thought, *like the past few months and this morning.*

"I'll only believe you if you've been seeing a little old lady in a black dress, black hat with a red flower in it. She's around town. That's the only thing that will help you now."

Colton couldn't believe it. He knew this man was his brother, his twin, but he had never known he had a sibling. The only parents he'd ever known were the Mitchells, upstanding citizens of Midland. "Oh, you mean Granny Spenser," he said. "Yeah, she's visited me several times today, too."

Colton never expected the reaction he received from the other man. He had only said the name unexpectedly, not even knowing he was going to say it, he just did.

"Right answer," the officer said, walking toward him. "I'm here to help you. She came to me this morning, twice, and the second time she said 'help him.' I reckon you're the one I'm supposed to help.

"None of this," he continued, spreading his hands, "us meeting here, obviously twins, now, at this particular time and place, none of this is coincidence. I only found out about Granny this morning, too, but I also believe she knows what she's doing. My uncle, George, insists that I have to do what she says."

"Your uncle?" Colton asked, incredulously. "Not George Spenser?"

"The one and only," the man replied. "So, what am I supposed to help you with?"

"At this point," Colton began, "you're probably here to help save the little girl that's missing. I feel she's still alive—"

Dan nodded his head, agreeing. Yes, he also knew she was still alive.

Colton saw his agreement, felt it, even. Maybe they had a chance with the two of them, two people trained as they were. Also, two people who would be thinking and reacting alike.

"She's not just any little girl," he continued. "She's *my* little girl."

"Yours?" the officer repeated. "But how—"

"I just found out this morning," Colton said. "Her mother was my high school sweetheart. To put it in a nutshell, when I went away to college, she was three months pregnant. She went to an aunt's in California, had the baby, told me to quit writing, stayed out there, and only returned to Midland a year ago."

"But she never told you?"

"No, she said she didn't want me to end up working in some factory in Fort Smith, resenting her and the baby for keeping me from college."

Dan nodded, understanding her reasoning. "It's happened," he said, holding out his hand. "I'm Dan, by the way."

"Colton," he said, shaking hands. "And, yeah, I know. But a daughter, and not knowing? That's why I'm here now. I know where the killer, the kidnapper, is. It's got to be the same one that's taken the children through the years. I know where it is, and I was just going to find it and kill it when you drove up. You might not want to help when you hear what I think."

Actually, Dan thought he was now prepared to hear anything. But what Colton had said was not lost on him. "You keep saying 'it.' So what's that supposed to mean?"

"Just that." Colton took a deep breath, watching his twin closely. There was no time right now to compare notes on families, to find out how they got separated. But he still wasn't sure what Dan might agree to do or not to do, Granny or no Granny.

Dan raised his eyebrows, waiting for a further explanation.

"I don't think we're dealing with a human here," Colton said.

"You don't, huh?" Dan replied with a straight face. He wondered how long, though, he might be able to keep it straight. *Oh, sure, why not? Hallucinations about little old ladies that speak then disappear into thin air, a twin showing up out of the blue. So, why not a non-human? What was so strange about that?* "So, are we talking alien here? Little green men from Mars, or what? Maybe it is really *The Alien.* Do you have Sigourney Weaver in your trunk, also?" Dan knew he was being sarcastic and knew it wasn't called for, but he couldn't help himself. Too much was happening too fast.

Colton shook his head. "You said you talked to your uncle this morning. Didn't he tell you I called?"

"Yes. No," Dan said, shaking his own head. "What time did you call?"

"About an hour and a half ago, maybe two," Colton replied. "I went to Fort Smith to get this stuff right after I talked to him. He's the one who helped me believe this thing with Granny Spenser. She's come to me twice this morning. Once she said 'you're the one.' It took a couple of hours, but I think I've figured out what I'm to do, that I'm the one to take care of this thing that's been taking children around here. The only difference is—and it doesn't fit the pattern—is the fact that, this time, Abigail has disappeared after only two years instead of the usual three."

"Yeah, that's different, all right," Dan agreed.

Colton looked at him questioningly. He was too

young to have been with the department for the first two or three disappearances.

Dan raised his eyebrows. "I came across the case accidentally a while back. Some old papers were in an old desk that I decided to restore. I got to looking at and reading about the disappearances. There were just too many coincidences."

"That's what I thought, too," Colton agreed. "We've been drawn here by powers beyond our control, it seems. Our best bet is to just flow with this thing. We might as well find out what we've got there."

"'There'?" Dan asked. "There, where?"

"The old Spenser House," Colton replied. "That's where it is, where it's been all this time, all these years."

"Yes, the trails all stopped right in front. The closeness of the house is what led me to arrest Otis Ledbetter. He's place is just down Elm Street, just across the field from the old house."

Colton started in surprise.. "Otis Ledbetter!" he repeated. "Otis? You didn't arrest Otis, did you? For these disappearances? I can't believe it. Otis wouldn't hurt a fly."

Dan managed to look contrite. He had already realized he had the wrong man. He had felt it for several days now.

"Why did you do that?" Colton asked. "Just proximity?"

"We found an old tennis shoe and lunch box in his

sheds. And they were identified as belonging to two of the girls that disappeared. The parents identified them, even after all this time. They also matched some evidence gathered at the time of the disappearances that was stored at the office."

"Oh, I have no doubt believing they belonged to the girls," Colton agreed. "Otis always was a scavenger, a real pack rat. Went around town picking up things people lost or put out by the trash. Otis might even have recognized them as belonging to the girls. You see," he continued, "we kids used to go up and down Elm Street all the time on our bikes, or even walking. Otis always waved to us, smiling. He was grown, or so it seemed, when I was a child but our parents had told us about him. They taught us to be nice, be kind to him, because he was simple minded. Sometimes we even stopped and petted his rabbits and kittens. He was always so proud to show us his rabbits."

Dan pictured in his mind a man cuddling and petting a rabbit.

"I know he thought of all of us, girls and boys alike, as his friends. Sometimes as a teenager, I would think about him and go visit. He had a good friend, Tom, who kept him company a lot. Tom just had a special feeling for Otis. Guess he saw him as his mission in life or something. But I would *never* have thought of Otis in connection with these missing children."

"There *was* evidence there," Dan replied. He felt the

need to defend his actions, to justify what he had done.

Colton thought about that. He nodded. "Yeah, I could see it, how you might think so. But not me, when I grew up with Otis."

"I didn't have that," Dan answered, still on the defensive.

"No, you didn't" Colton agreed. "Where's Otis now?" he asked, nodding his head in the direction of the Ledbetter place.

"Actually, he's not there."

"Oh?" Colton asked, raising his eyebrows.

"Sebastian County Jail," came the reply.

"No," Colton said, disbelievingly. "He's probably so stressed out there, he doesn't know who he is. His familiar routine was his security blanket."

"It gets worse," Dan admitted.

"Worse than jail?" Colton asked. He pictured the Cook County jail. That place could be a real zoo at times!

"'Fraid so," Dan said, as he pulled on an ear—a habit Colton himself did whenever he was nervous or upset, which wasn't very often.

Colton just looked at him, waiting.

"The jury's out right now. They're to reach a verdict by Monday."

"Verdict? For what?" Colton couldn't believe what he was hearing. First, the missing children, then spirits appearing, talking even. Then discovering he had a daughter, but she was missing, then a twin. Then to hear that poor old Otis Ledbetter had been accused and brought to trial for the crimes. What could possibly happen next?

"Kidnapping. Murder. But just on two of the cases, the ones we had the evidence for."

"You gotta be kidding!" Colton exclaimed. "Not Otis."

They just stared at each other. Each knew what the other was thinking, but there didn't seem to be much to say about it.

"Maybe we're just in time to save him from what to him would literally be a fate worse than death," Colton offered, speaking first. "Look at what I bought at the army surplus store."

He led the way to his truck and opened it, revealing several weapons and protective gear that Dan recognized. "Are we going up against one person, or an army?" he asked.

Each item had no great potential danger within itself, but put it all together, the artillery looked like an arsenal for one of those survival camps, the ones that taught guerilla tactics as a form of offense. There was a flamethrower—heavy-duty, militaristic type. If it came to it, if fire turned out to be the means he had to use to destroy whatever he found, Colton wanted a steady, dependable, uninterrupted stream for as long as it took to defeat the monster. And Colton had begun to think of whatever it was as a monster. He knew it was going to be something supernatural, something beyond his wildest imagination.

His worst nightmare was about to come true. He knew that if it weren't for the fact that Abigail was in there, and he was sure *it* was in the cellar, if it weren't for her, he might, just might, lose his courage and decide it was too much for him and just let the thing be. But, no. On the other hand, he knew he could never let it go. And now he had help. He knew Dan would never give up, either. One child every three years was one child too many, had been from the beginning.

And they had to know what was there. Even if, in their chosen profession, their sworn allegiance to perform their duty had not been there, Colton and Dan would have felt the call to fight evil, in whatever form it might take.

And evil it was! Granny's presence and George's testimony as to what had happened years ago revealed this. Colton just hoped he was strong enough to stand up to it when the time came to do so. He hoped that when he faced it, he didn't do anything stupid like pee his pants or something, perhaps out of fear.

Dan was thinking somewhat along the same lines. Until this morning, whenever the men or one lady on his staff got around to talking about UFOs, intelligent life on other planets, or visitations from other dimensions, he usually just laughed and had something cute, but definitely unbelieving, to say. Even now, he thought that, deep down within himself, they were about to face a psychopath. Some sicko who had been a hermit or loner for so long he went completely bananas every three years or so. And now he was just speeding up his timetable.

Maybe it was someone who had been in Vietnam. He had heard that many of those men could not mentally handle whatever they had seen or been forced to do there. He knew, in his own work, that there were times he just wanted to close his eyes and never open them again. Those were times when law enforcement officials found a mutilated, mangled body, perhaps of what had been beautiful young lady. Only someone with a completely twisted mind could do some of the things he had seen, and those people usually felt that what they did was for the good of all mankind.

But nothing in nature, in the animal or plant kingdom, could do anything compared to what some humans were capable of doing to other humans. Deliberate, premeditated acts of cruelty and violence were unknown to animals. If they seemed vicious in their attacks on other animals, they were simply acting as they were programmed in nature to do. Survival of the fittest was the rule in the wild.

But where animals could not reason and choose, thus becoming responsible for their actions, humans could. So those humans who turned on other humans had no excuse for their actions.

Dan turned back to the trunk, bringing his thoughts back to the matter at hand. After lifting out the flamethrower, he drew in a long whistle. He looked quickly up at Colton.

"You really have no idea what you're up against, do you?"

Colton returned his look, knowing he could not fool this man.

"Not really," he replied then paused.

"And?" Dan asked, seeing there was more to this story. He looked down The Lane, as if he could see the old house, although it could not be seen from the beginning of The Lane.

"I don't know," Colton answered simply. "I only feel there's something. Just be still a minute and listen."

Dan stood very still. He didn't know what he was supposed to be listening to or for.

"I don't hear a thing," he said, after several minutes.

"Exactly," Colton said. "That's part of it."

"What's part of it, and part of what?"

"There are no animals here. Just look around and listen again."

Dan stood still a second time, listening and glancing around. Colton was right. No birds flew in the air or sang in the trees. No mice or earth animals stirred in the underbrush. He looked at Colton questioningly.

Colton nodded in response.

"Its food for years now has been small animals, things it could lure through a small hole in the outside cellar door. Or, they might even have wandered in accidentally." He shrugged. "Who knows? Who can know?"

"And have you thought of something else?" Dan asked. "What if this *is* an alien. Don't you think there are scientists who would want to have it captured alive, would want to study it, and perhaps learn to communicate with it?"

"This intelligence, if it has any, has been killing children, for God's sake!" Colton exclaimed.

"That's just it," Dan interrupted. "What if God did create it? What if it's just here by mistake?"

Colton had just had a similar conversation awhile earlier with Marsha. He felt he was ready to be on the other side, now. But he had made his decision.

"I want to kill it before it kills my little girl," he replied, bending over the full trunk, trying to decide just what to start putting on first.

"Are you going to help, or not?" he asked Dan, looking up at him.

"Do you really think it's evil?" Dan asked.

"Our Granny thought so, didn't she? She even made her family leave a beautiful home because she sensed the evil of it. You saw her—she spoke to you. Are you doing to doubt her?"

"I don't doubt Granny," Dan said, "only the idea that it's automatically evil, in and of itself. All creatures have a basic instinct for survival. Perhaps we can assume an alien creature has the same primal need."

Colton straightened up, looking at his brother.

"What you're saying is this thing doesn't even know it's committing an evil, an atrocity, against us as humans? That its thought process may be so different that it has no concept of evil?"

"Yes, or any concept of right or wrong, or moral or immoral, not as we know it, at least. Our country, and, yes, most of the world, has a concept of God and laws that have been handed down for centuries, since the beginning of this world. What if another world, or worlds, even, have no such concept? Would that make this creature's actions evil, just because we were judging it on our own notions and teachings?"

"You mean it might not have God?" Colton asked.

"Or *a* god, or *gods*," Dan replied. "Or, it might have a god with completely different teachings because its needs are so different. You can't rush in there, not knowing."

"Try me," Colton answered. "With the life of my daughter at stake, it can have a hundred different theologies or philosophies. If there's a chance Abigail's alive, and I have to kill this…this…*thing*…to get to her, then I *will* kill it! And if it's simply a psycho, a human being with no conscience, possessed by evil, then I'll destroy that, too, because it becomes something less than human by what it's done."

"But you're pretty well convinced there's another species there, though, aren't you?" Dan asked.

"I don't know, I really don't. But if I've accepted

that Granny, or Granny's spirit, is still roaming around, not able to rest until this evil is destroyed, then I accept the fact that there is something there. And it seems I'm the one who's supposed to kill it, and you're supposed to help me."

Colton had been lifting things out of the trunk as he spoke. Now he stopped and looked up at Dan.

"Well?" he asked.

Dan knew he was going to help his brother. He had never doubted that. He just wanted to be sure that whatever they did was right. He had thought that perhaps destroying whatever it was might not the answer. But he wouldn't know that for sure until they encountered it. He started helping Colton lift out the weapons. They had to decide who was going to carry what and how they were going to proceed.

"Wait," Dan said.

"What?" Colton asked, straightening up.

"I just wondered. How were you going to carry all this by yourself?" he asked, his arm moving to include all the items they had placed on the ground.

"With determination, I guess." Colton grinned. "I just knew I wanted every kind of weapon I could get. There's no telling which, or what combinations, will destroy it."

"If it can be destroyed," Dan said quietly.

They looked at each other.

"Yeah," Colton agreed, "if it *can* be destroyed."

Several minutes went by as the men unloaded the vehicle.

"Look, do you know what you've done here?" Dan asked, looking at the equipment they had laid out on the ground.

Colton paused at the back door, his hand on the handle. He had more equipment, which he thought of as weapons, on the back seat. "Sure, I bought a little of everything."

"No, I mean you have *two* of everything. Look! Here are two gas masks, two flamethrowers, two shotguns!"

"You're kidding!" Colton responded, as he walked back that way.

"You said your girlfriend rode to Fort Smith with you. Did you plan on her coming out here, doing battle with you against this thing?

"No, of course not," Colton said. "That thought never entered my mind. I would not have considered it. I took her home before coming here this time."

The two men looked at each other, both thinking the same thing. Now Colton understood why Marsha had kept asking about helping him. It was not chance or circumstance that he and Dan were both in this place at the same time.

They knew and acknowledged a force beyond themselves that drew them here.

Colton had planned for Dan being here, helping, without even knowing he had. "I wasn't even aware I had bought two of everything. You know what this means, don't you?"

Dan nodded. "Yeah," he said. "Let's go."

Chapter 31

Colton and Dan Go Hunting

The two men moved silently, each aware of the vast and complete silence around them.

It was a dead, unearthly silence.

If the leaves in the trees had not been making a gentle rustling sound occasionally as the wind moved them against each other, there would have been no sound at all. Although heavily armed, these two men were trained for stealth. Often, not only their lives, but the lives of their fellow officers, depended on such quiet and caution.

Colton had warned Dan about his coming here earlier, his having spotted the sealed-up inside basement door and finding the outside entrance, hidden behind years and years of ivy and undergrowth. But his earlier visit may also have warned whatever was there of his presence. If it were more animal than anything, then Colton would have left his scent and perhaps even now it smelled his second coming. If more human, it would no doubt be watching for his return. If neither, then Colton could not imagine what it might be doing in preparation for his coming.

Such a murderous beast had to be slain. No, Colton did not think of it as murder. This was a beast, an animal, to be slain mercilessly as it had slain the children. Even if it had started out as, had once perhaps been, human, its actions had rendered it more bestial than human. And a rabid beast had to be destroyed.

Both men kept a watchful eye on the house and the woods surrounding it as they approached the house from the front. They slowly circled around. Each having taken one side, they met at the back.

Nothing had moved or made a sound in the woods around them. Nothing had been disturbed since Colton had been here a few hours earlier. The boards he had ripped off and tossed away were still where they had landed. His footprints in the deep dust were still apparent from the back door to the basement door. There were not that many steps, for Colton remembered going across the distance in a few quick, long strides, only enough to allow him to pick up the barrette, turn, and get out as rapidly as possible.

The men paused at the back door, listening for any

movement or noise in the house. The silence itself was palpable. It almost felt alive, moving across the face as a breath of air, chilling the soul. They moved forward, slowly, putting down part of the equipment they had brought, but keeping it within reaching distance at all times.

Colton had warned Dan that the first thing they would have to do was get into the cellar. They had talked about going through the door at the back of the house, but dismissed that as a possible entrance point. Having to bend and enter the room would have put them at a physical disadvantage that neither was willing to face.

Not really knowing what they were going up against was bad enough. They wanted every advantage they could think of, just as Colton had tried to think of every defensive weapon he could, not knowing what they needed.

Getting through the inside door was not going to be easy. At that point, they would both be vulnerable to attack. The door had been sealed off from this side. Could something get out another way?

No. Nothing. Nothing normal, that is.

On the other hand, neither could anyone, or anything, go down this way without leaving tracks or prints in the dust. What had Granny Spenser started, and then became afraid of? he wondered. Whatever it was, it was the only thing in her life that had frightened her so profoundly. At first, it had affected her to the point that she had this cellar boarded up. That would have put the family in a serious situation, for then they would not have had space to store their garden produce and canned goods. This food always carried the family through the winter.

Next, whatever it was had influenced her to the extent that she insisted the whole family abandon what was a beautiful home. A family of six simply packed up and moved away because the old lady said so.

Shortly after beginning the task of breaking open the inside basement door wide enough for the men to fit through, Colton and Dan were sweating profusely. Both refused to remove any of the protective clothing. One watched one way, one the other as they used crowbars and hammers to remove nails and the boards that had been nailed firmly in place many years before. That's why the door had been perfectly flush with the wall, able to be completely sealed when covered over with wallpaper.

Also, the crevices had been filled in with paint, this paint acting like a strong glue to hold the door and boards in place.

They had to chisel and use an awl in the cracks, breaking the old, dried, struck paint off. Dan had helped a friend redo an old house several years back, where the windows had been stuck shut with paint when the previous owner had painted the window frames. This was many times worse than those stuck windows. Then, the owner had accidentally, and inadvertently, allowed the paint to stick the windowpane in place. In this case, it was a deliberate and thorough application of the paint for the purpose of keeping the door shut.

Certainly, whatever they would soon be facing had plenty of time to be prepared for them. Even moving as quickly as they could, Dan felt they were moving in slow motion. They were making so much noise as they worked, that someone from the town was sure to show up at any minute, asking what they were doing. But no one appeared, and the two men continued pulling out boards, tossing them aside quickly as they came off.

Personally, they were silent, even when the crowbar or hammer slipped, crushing a finger. They were unwilling to give the enemy any advantage over them. An outcry of pain of any kind would have been used against them later.

Colton knew part of his sweating was due to his anxiety and, yes, fear, of what might be coming. Every scary movie he had seen flashed through his mind—every monster, zombie, or creature from the mind of such who developed those images for movies.

Finally, with grunts on the part of both men, the last board came off the frame.

They straightened, taking deep breaths, getting their thoughts and equilibrium back in balance. Both felt the tension of the other. Both willed themselves to relax. They remained still and silent. There was nothing they could say to each other. Both were ready, mentally and physically, all senses acutely attuned and aware of any movement or sound from the room below.

Colton reached his hand out and gripped the old white, glass knob of the door. It was one of those with a white marble surface, above a "skeleton" key-type lock hole.

Fitting, he thought. *A skeleton key would seem appropriate, somehow.*

Was it locked? It would take them longer than ever to get to their destination if the door were locked.

The knob turned in his hand as he pulled the door outward. He thought at first that the door was not going to budge farther, was indeed locked, but then he felt it give.

A few more hard tugs, and it began to open slowly. The wood had swollen over the years from a hole in the roof above it, a hole that had allowed the rain to soak the door and the wood to swell.

But at last, with a final creak, it swung wide open.

A blast of cold air swept over them as a stale stench rose from the depths below. The men turned immediately to put on their gas masks. Colton had told Dan about the odor earlier, so Dan did not hesitate to put the mask on. Neither man was willing to breathe the nauseating odor any more than was necessary. It might or might not be toxic.

In silence, they picked up the equipment they had brought and arranged it on their bodies. A lot of the equipment would provide protection, which they knew would be just as important as their attack.

The stairs were dark, as Colton had known they would be. But there was a faint spattering of light at the bottom, a dim glow that might have been given off by a small window on the opposite side of the room.

Colton knew this minute amount of light came from the small hole in the outside door of the cellar, the small hole made by the bodies of many small animals. Those small creatures, hapless victims, were going to help the men now. Nothing had helped the animals at the time they would have entered through the small opening. Their small lives would have been snuffed out mercilessly, mindlessly. Now, they would help destroy their predator.

After signaling to Dan to remain where he was in the old kitchen, Colton stepped quickly but cautiously down three stairs and flattened himself against the wall. When the door had swung completely open, he had noticed the wall on his right, a wooden handrail on the left. The second rail down was missing, which warned Colton of the condition of the boards. Flattening himself as much as possible against the wall, he stood still, listening. Another blast of cold air assaulted him as he stepped through the doorway. It not only chilled his body, but his very soul as well.

He knew, for a split second, that, as he stepped through the doorway, he had been silhouetted against the light from behind the door. If anyone had wanted to open fire on him, then would have been the time. But he doubted the danger would come from a gun. This psycho had practiced stealth and cunning for many, many years now, and he was not likely to do anything at this point to draw attention to himself.

For who knew? A chance hunter nearby or someone choosing to take Spenser's Lane as a shortcut somewhere might hear a gunshot. Then, of course, the game would be over.

No, definitely not a gun.

Colton was more in danger from a silent, surprise attack and that's why he paused to listen. The settling of the boards, a creak from an old piece of tin flapping on the porch, the wind itself whipping around the corner of the house were the only sounds he heard.

He was trained to count. After forty seconds, having heard nothing more, he decided to descend the darkened staircase into the dank, cool area below.

While in high school, one of Colton's favorite stories had been that of Beowulf. He pictured himself now, as Beowulf must have been—clad in chain mail, helmet, with a sword at his side. Colton was clad much the same way, as modern as his weapons might be.

But he knew, like Beowulf against Grendel, that the battle would be won with courage. The victory in battle would probably also go to the swiftest. Surprise might be his best weapon, giving him the advantage over whatever man or beast he was to face.

And he knew it would be a fight to the finish.

If he did not rescue Abigail, he would die trying.

Colton wondered if, like Grendel, there might be more than one beast in the cellar, in its liar, as it were. Maybe only one, the male or female, did the hunting, a hunting that occasionally included a little girl. Maybe this one brought back food for others. If so, then Colton certainly needed Dan's help, no matter whom or what had told Dan to help.

How many more creatures of the night, in particular, lived and flourished in the world, in parts of the earth, perhaps, where no human dared to wander, or, if any had wandered there, by chance or design, how many had not returned?

For centuries, there had been tales of creatures that came forth from the sea depths, from the deep forests, from rocks and dark shadows. These creatures, cruel and ghostly, were supposed to have looked for victims among hapless humans.

Man never understood these preternatural creatures, whose natures were so chaotic that the human mind could not comprehend them. And more and more, humans were intruding on their domains, on their feeding grounds. There were many unexplained disappearances in history. The Roanoke, Virginia, colony was one. Did creatures such as this once watch these unsuspecting colonists with greedy feral eyes glinting, clawed hands curled, waiting for the cover of darkness to pounce on their prey?

Those were hard and lonely times. The night pierced only by smoky lamps or tallow candles, that gave out only a small circle of light. Did creatures such as this watch furtively as daylight turned to twilight and most humans chose to enter their cabins, boarding up doors and windows as nighttime fell—choosing to be in out of the all-embracing dark that would have taken over their world. What creatures of the forest surrounded the colonists as they slept? What ones still roamed around Midland? If people were fortunate, they heard nothing while they slept, not even the occasional hooting of an owl or the sounds of other nocturnal animals. For the night could bring chaos in the world, as it still did in the inner city.

Is there a route by which forgotten creatures, monsters, or aliens, if you will, could enter into this world? And once they found that portal, can they return to their own world, or are they doomed to live in this one, as foreboding and sinister to them, as theirs would be to us? Have these children simply been seized by some immortal creature that accidentally found a portal? Perhaps they were seized by crooked claws and forced to go with the monsters, back to the realms of the deep from which they came.

And what about the manifestations of Granny Spenser? Could he and Dan both have hallucinated the same things, at different places and at different times?

People had believed in Granny's power, and that of her father before her, for many, many years. Who was there to say she did not exist in another world, one parallel, yet unseen, by this one?

What about dreams? Did the spirit leave the body and travel to some distant world, only to have to return before dawn? Many cultures throughout the centuries had believed just that—which the spirit left the body at night, fought among themselves then returned.

Even the most religious of mankind had its stories, its concoctions of spirits, goblins, troll, but especially spirits, which could enter any form they wished.

Marsha had not been willing to believe, but Colton did believe. Did this monster, also, shamble through the undergrowth, from time to time, using speed and claws, to catch and tear its prey? Its prey had obviously been the hapless creatures of the forest—rabbits, mice, even the domesticated dogs and cats of the townspeople. Was it old, having been an inhabitant of the earth long before man? Unlike most creatures of prey, however, this monster did not wait in the shadows or for night to cover its stealth-like movements. Obviously, these children had disappeared in daylight. Had it rushed at these children, crushing their bodies in giant talons and cracking bones with oversized jaws?

Why hadn't the men or bloodhounds ever found pools or even drops of blood?

What satiated the beast? It seemed content to feed on human flesh only once every three years and then it preferred the tender young skin and bones of children. Why weren't other bodies found anywhere, gruesomely mangled or torn apart?

Colton shook his head, bringing his thoughts back to the matter at hand. Beckoning to Dan, he started toward the unknown. Slower than ever, they took one step at a time down the short staircase to the dark, dank recess of the cellar. It was cold down here, even though it was high summer outside. It wasn't just cool, it was so cold that Colton was thankful for the insulated jumpsuit he had bought—was grateful for both of them he had bought!

Dan stepped on a loose board that creaked loudly, but did not dislodge. He quickly regained his balance. Colton had stepped on the other side of the board, so Dan decided to follow his steps exactly. Although the men had hardhats with lights built in them, shining brightly forward, it was still difficult to see every nook and corner clearly. One false step and they could be in a world of hurt.

The cruelty of this beast might seem to be beyond the comprehension of some, but not Colton, who had seen some pretty weird stuff going down in Cook County. He was prepared for anything as he stepped off the bottom step and moved aside for Dan. At least that's what he had told himself. He was not prepared for the sight that met them from the corner of the room in the glow of their headlamps.

Cannibalism! Could it be? Colton could hardly believe what he was seeing. No wonder the odors around this place had been so awful. No wonder the smell was something he had not quite experienced before. The crazy thought went through his mind about whether the monster that did this cooked the children or ate them raw!

Jeez! What a thought to have!

The men felt faint, barely able to believe what their eyes were telling them was in front of them. They were not sure what they had expected, but certainly not this. At least Dan had not been prepared for this. He had been ready for a flesh-and-blood psychopath, perhaps mad and raving, but nevertheless seemingly human. Seeing the bones and skulls of humans put the psycho less than human. People who did this were definitely in a category by themselves.

Then Colton's eye caught something at the opposite wall, and he thought he was again seeing things—had wished something so badly that he was imagining it to be true.

There was a girl, leaning up with her back against the wall, seeming to be held there by nothing at all, but a faint movement of Colton's head caused the light to shimmer on a web, so thin it was almost undetectable.

Fishing line? Was she being held upright there by fishing line? Her eyes were closed and she made no movement. She had not acknowledged their presence.

Yet Colton knew she was alive.

He also knew it was Abigail. Even if he had not seen her photos, he would have known it was Abigail. She was alive. Thank God, she was alive. His joy at seeing her was so complete, so overwhelming, that for a second his mind was taken off their other purpose for being there.

He brought his attention back from the figure against the wall and turned more fully to view the rest of the room. He instinctively knew that, if no one had pounced or shot at them by now, it probably wouldn't happen. The element of surprise was now gone from the moment.

They both turned every way, shining their lights into every corner and crevice of the basement. Obviously, the kidnapper was not here.

"Get her," Dan said. "I'll guard you as you get her out. Is she alive?"

As Dan began speaking, Colton was already heading toward Abigail. She was held with a thin, fishing-line-type wire. He touched her throat.

"Yes, she's alive. Looks like she's okay," he responded. He never knew he could feel such relief. Many emotions flooded over him. He would have to sort them out later.

The line was easily cut and torn off her. He gently lifted her up in his arms, making her as comfortable as his equipment would permit.

"Good. Let's go, then. I don't want to be here when this man comes back. We'll bring in some more men and clean this place out. I bet, though, we'll find those skulls are those of the missing children."

"Yeah, I bet so, too," Colton said. He started up the

stairs with Abigail in his arms. "Freakin' cannibalism. I can't believe it."

Both men were still shocked by what they had discovered here. Colton kept mumbling to himself about cannibals. Dan just hoped he made it up the stairs and into the fresh air before he tossed his cookies. Even that would be hard to do with the gas mask on.

As soon as they reached the outside, they threw off their masks, both taking large, long gulps of the fresh air.

Colton laid Abigail gently down in the grass beside The Lane.

Thank God!

He slumped, leaning back on his heels, took one of her hands, and started rubbing up and down her hand and arm. Tears were rolling down his cheeks, unbidden and unchecked.

"Abigail! Abigail! Wake up!" he cried, so relieved at finding her alive, he could not stop his tears.

She moaned and turned her head sideways.

"Abigail, darling! Wake up!" he repeated, rubbing her upper arms, hoping to restore circulation.

Her eyelids fluttered and she opened her eyes briefly but had to close them again. "Mama?" she whispered, weakly.

"Your mother is waiting for you, Abigail. Don't worry. You're safe now. Your mother is waiting for you."

"Good," she whispered, closing her eyes again.

She was asleep. But it was a regular sleep this time.

Her pulse and breathing were regular. Colton watched her for another minute, holding her wrist, checking her pulse. It grew stronger.

Yes, this was just sleep. He knew she was going to be okay. He laid her gently back.

Dan had walked a little way from them, into the bushes a few feet away. He had been unable to keep from upchucking.

Suddenly, from the tall grass on the opposite side of The Lane, a large hairy figure jumped up and rushed toward Colton. The figure made no sound and Colton only saw it coming because he had started to turn around. He barely caught a glimpse of it before the man had charged into him, knocking him to the ground on his back. He…it?…stayed on top of Colton, obviously going for his throat with his teeth. It took Colton a few seconds to react but when he did it was with a vengeance. This thing smelled just like the basement. Here was their killer, their cannibal. Colton heaved with all his might, arching his back. He succeeded in throwing the man off him, knocking him sideways and off balance. Colton immediately rolled the opposite way.

He was preparing for another attack when he heard gunfire. The gunfire was close, no more than a few feet from him.

It was Dan firing. Colton felt the air from the bullets as they whizzed past him. He dared not move.

Dan did not quit firing until he heard the "click,

click" of his revolver. He had emptied his whole clip into the attacker.

He bent down, rolled the man over, grimaced, and stepped back. Not only was the smell of the man overpowering, but the grotesqueness of his features was repulsive.

They could see he had elongated arms ending with over-sized hands. The hands themselves ended in long, curled-under claws. Colton couldn't think of them as fingernails. They were definitely claws. He wondered if they had ever been cut in the entire life of this creature. His facial features were distorted, his lips on one side twisting up the side of his face. He didn't seem to have a nose, only two holes were a nose should have been. His ears were two holes on each side of his head. They could see this although the man's thin, long hair hung down below his shoulders.

"What is it?" Dan asked in a choking voice, then cleared his throat.

"I'm not sure," Colton responded.

They stood for several more minutes, just staring at the figure on the ground.

"Deformed? Mutant?" Dan asked, when he found his voice again.

"That and more," Colton agreed. "Where did something like this come from? How could it be here all this time and no one around here not know it?"

Dan just shook his head. He knew Colton didn't really expect an answer from him. Hell, he didn't have any answers.

"I'll call for help," he said, heading toward the top of The Lane to his patrol car. "You staying here?" he asked Colton.

"Yeah, I'll stay. Make sure the body doesn't go any-where. Abigail's okay, I think, but you might call nine-one-one just in case. And you might give Marsha a call when you get a chance. And..." His voice trailed off. He just couldn't continue.

"One thing at a time, pal," Dan said. "I'll be right back."

Colton knelt down beside Abigail again. He took his shirt off, putting it gently under her head, and positioned himself where he could watch the body while he waited for Dan to return. Logically, Colton knew the man was dead, but what he was looking at was not logical, so he kept a watch.

He tenderly stroked Abigail's arm with one hand. His relief at finding her alive was beyond words. Tears again sprang into his eyes, and he made no effort to stop them. He didn't even care that he was still crying when he heard Dan return. He was still crying when he heard a siren in the distance.

The first deputy to arrive at the scene took one look at the body and backed several feet away. He looked questioningly at his sheriff. Dan just silently shook his head.

Colton turned to Dan. They were beginning to hear more sirens.

"Thanks," he said, touching Dan's shoulder. He couldn't say more.

"Later, brother," Dan replied.

As soon as two more of his men arrived, doing the same double-take the first deputy had on seeing both men, obviously twins, Dan and his deputies headed toward the old house. They would collect all the "evidence" they could.

They knew, however, that they had solved the mystery of what had happened to the children over the past twenty years. The question would remain of who this person was and how he happened to be here.

Colton turned, squatting down to pick Abigail up in his arms. He was now in a hurry to get her home to Marsha. But more than that he just wanted to touch her, feel that she was, indeed, still alive, unharmed by this monster. He reached his car and put her in the seat beside him, strapping her into the seatbelt.

In case she regained consciousness, he wanted her beside him. She did not know him, of course. He would need to reassure her.

He was her father. His love was beyond words.

Chapter 32

Old Man Ogden Adds to the Tale

As soon as Colton left him the last time, Old Man Ogden had reached for his can of tobacco. He slowly started rolling a cigarette, as if in slow motion.

He was silent.

There were customers, a few locals, in the store. It was not until they had been gone for a while that Bob Adams, the owner, noticed something was different, something wrong. At first he couldn't put his finger on what it was. Then it dawned on him that Jim Ogden wasn't talking. He was not talking to him, anyone, or even to himself, which was normally the case.

Jim Ogden had started talking sometime around 1957 and had not shut up since, even when customers were all over the store. Most people, who were local townspeople and knew him, stopped to talk to him a minute, at least to say hello, but it didn't seem to matter to Jim Ogden if anyone was there or not.

He just simply rattled on and on.

Adams had heard that voice for so many years now that he had quit listening years ago. Ogden's voice had become a normal part of the environment, so much so that, now that it had stopped, Adams knew it was not normal.

This silence was different.

Something had to be wrong.

He walked over to the old man, stopped beside him. Ogden's eyes were closed. This worried Adams. Heart attack! That was his first thought. He put his hand out and gently touched Ogden's shoulder. Ogden jerked, opening his eyes, causing Adams to jump back a step.

"You okay, Jim?" Adams asked.

Ogden looked up at his lifelong friend.

"Right as rain, old friend."

Ogden's eyes were clear, bright, as he looked steadily at his friend.

Adams saw the intelligence he knew had been there once, long ago, before Jim started rattling about Granny Spenser, other babies, and such.

"I was worried. You quit talking, and, well, you haven't…I mean…you always…" Adams didn't quite know how to put what he meant into words, not wanting to hurt his friend's feelings.

"Talk," Ogden said, supplying the word for him. "Yeah, I know. I always talk. Been talking for years now, hoping someone would listen and do something about it. Decided long ago I'd keep talking 'til someone *did* listen and understand. Well, young Mitchell listened and understood what I was saying and is doing something."

The old man slowly got up from his rocking chair and started toward the front door of the store. Adams just stood there, unable to move, staring after him. For the first time since he'd known him, Ogden had spoken clearly, slowly, instead of the fast, constant mumbling he usually did. But the words he said still did not make any sense to Adams. Understood what? Was Ogden really aware of all the talking he had done? Had he really known what he was saying all these years? By what he just said, and in the way he said it, he had been aware. But where was he going now? For more years than Adam could remember, Ogden was at the door when he opened up and only left the store in the evening when he closed up.

Every day, Ogden bought a sandwich for lunch, which Adams made for him from his meat case. He never left the store. He was there six days a week, while the store was open.

Adams watched as Ogden took a seat in one of the

chairs on the front porch of the general store. As Ogden settled himself and reached for his tobacco and papers, Adams continued to watch for several minutes. The old man was still quiet. This was not his usual behavior and it worried Adams.

When nothing stranger happened than Ogden's having moved from the inside of the store to the outside, Adams shook his head and went to his stockroom.

Crazy old man! he thought. But he still had a great affection for him. You didn't listen to and help watch out for someone all these years without caring.

On the porch, Ogden was content to sit and smoke, waiting. He was content because he knew the purpose of his life had been fulfilled, was being fulfilled as he sat there, and he was satisfied.

He sensed someone standing beside him. Then he felt a hand touch his shoulder. He reached one of his bony, gnarled hands up and laid it on top of the hand on his shoulder, gently patting it.

"It's over," a voice whispered, barely audible. It was a voice out of time, out of space, a voice so thin it might have been part of the air.

A voice both Colton and Dan would have recognized, Colton from his childhood as well as now.

Ogden looked up at the person standing there and gave her hand a few final pats, taking his hand away and laying it in his lap.

"Yep. You can rest now," he replied.

"Yes," agreed the voice, even more breathy and part of the air.

Ogden actually felt the relief and joy in that simple word. The hand stayed on Old Man Ogden's shoulder for a few more long seconds, and then it was gone.

Ogden sensed the presence leaving. He would not see his friend again. But that was all right. Her purpose had been fulfilled, also. It had just taken her longer, that's all. But she could rest at last. It wouldn't be long now. He rested his head on the back of the chair.

After a while, he heard the county fire truck start up, the siren blaring. He lifted his head and turned it to the right.

He nodded.

Yep, it was over.

He saw a car approaching.

As Colton drew near the old man, he slowed his pace and stopped the car in front of the store.

"Reckon everything's okay now, young Mitchell," Ogden said, as he leaned forward in his chair. It was not a question, simply a statement of fact.

"Reckon so," Colton replied.

Colton had tears in his eyes, unable to form the words to thank this man.

"No need," Ogden said, raising his hand, seeming to understand Colton's thoughts.

"She okay?" he asked, nodding toward the girl.

"Yes, thanks to you," Colton managed, before his voice caught in his throat again.

Old Man Ogden waved his hand again, nodding as he leaned back in the chair.

"Take care, now," he said.

"Yes, sir," Colton said, as he turned to continue up the street to the Masons', to his love and the mother of this child, his daughter.

He turned at the corner and looked back to where Old Man Ogden still sat in the chair. He would come back later and tell him all about it, because he knew the old man was the only one who would believe him, believe what they had discovered at the old Spenser House.

He vowed to do something special for the old man.

But the old man didn't need anything else done for him. Just like Granny, his purpose had been fulfilled.

He closed his eyes with a sigh.

Epilogue

A Family

Colton and Marsha sat in the swing on Marsha's front porch. They gently rocked back and forth, their legs swinging together in perfect harmony. They held hands.

They touched often now, each not wanting to let the other out of sight.

Dan sat on the other side of the porch. He was leaning back in a metal lawn chair. His hands were linked together on his stomach. His feet were up on the rail of the porch, one ankle crossed over the other.

Abigail was sitting cross-legged out in the yard, playing with her new puppy.

Colton had taken a lot of time and care choosing that dog. They had gone to three different animal shelters before they found the perfect pet. This puppy had three inches of white on top of its head and white on the tip of its tail.

Dan was the first to break the silence. He really didn't want to. It was so peaceful here. It was the perfect domestic scene in perfect Small-town, USA.

Peace would finally come to this town.

Dozens of men and women had combed the woods and meadows around the old Spenser House and the Ledbetter place. They found several piles of bones that were tested to be those of dogs. The forensic test results on the two skulls found in the cellar of the old house matched them to two of the missing girls. They couldn't completely match all the bones they found piled in the corner. The search teams had tried to find other bodies, graves, or anything that would help solve the mystery but no graves were ever found.

It would take a long, long time for people to forget what had been discovered here. It had not been right around here for many, many years, however, and that was what they needed to talk about now.

"Old Man Ogden knew, didn't he?" Dan asked.

He didn't have to explain what he was referring to.

"Yeah, he knew all along who was out there, who was kidnapping those girls. I think, though, that part of the time he forced himself not to think about it and that made him appear crazy and talk crazy. I think, also, that some of the time he just simply forgot all about it. When he did think about it, he was probably so guilt-ridden, he wouldn't admit to anything. I mean, how could he admit to knowing about something like this all these years and never having told anyone? It almost puts him as an accessory after the fact. But what can you do with a ninety-five-year-old man who doesn't know who he is half the time?"

"Yeah, I know what you mean," Dan agreed.

"Why do you think he was there that night?"

"At the Ledbetter place? At Otis's birth?" Colton referred to it as "Otis's birth" because he did not want to think of the other.

"Yeah."

"Possibly he was just a friend of the Ledbetters. He had a car. Maybe he thought they would need help, or something."

"Do you think he had anything to do with Ledbetter's suicide?"

"I really don't think so. I think when Ledbetter saw an ugly, deformed mass of a baby come out of his wife's body, it was too much for him. Remember the mayor said he had a problem, anyway. I think he just couldn't handle anymore."

They were each lost in his and her own thoughts for a few minutes. Each wondered what would bring someone to suicide. There were no answers for that. No one ever knew what was in another person's head.

The only sounds were the creaking of the swing as it went back and forth and Abigail's squeal of delight as the puppy crawled all over her, licking her face.

"So why do you think Ogden never said anything through the years? Or even did nothing? I mean, he could have written an anonymous note or something to us, or to anybody, for that matter," Dan said.

Dan was more or less musing to himself. He didn't really expect a reply.

"If you want my *personal* opinion," Colton began, "I do have one. I realize a lot of the conclusions we've drawn about this whole matter have been based on opinion and speculation. We could piece it together pretty well, though. But I have a different opinion about the old man."

He fell silent. Both Marsha and Dan remained quiet. They knew Colton would continue when he was ready.

"What I think is—and you can tell me if I'm really in left field with this—what I think is that he was in love with Granny Spenser. Probably had been all his life."

Again there was silence as they all thought about this.

"Well, that *is* a good theory. What makes you think that?"

"He was there that night when Granny helped with the Ledbetter delivery. Why he was there we may never know. Maybe he was her assistant at births. I have a feeling he's still not telling *all* he knows."

Dan nodded agreement. He had the same feeling. "He probably never will tell all, even if he remembers everything. Maybe he was also a friend of the Ledbetters. But I think Granny asked him to come help her. Probably he saw the first baby born and saw Granny put it aside, discard it, if you will. He may even have told her to do it. A baby that deformed back then probably had little chance of survival. I'm sure it was Granny's intention to let it die. Also, you have to know that a lot of folk around here back then would have thought a baby like that was a sign of the devil. I would bet a year's salary that Granny thought so. People around these parts have always been superstitious, at least on the whole. They certainly would have back in the 'thirties. They believed in those things like don't let a black cat cross your path or don't walk under a ladder, that sort of thing."

"Well, your Uncle George said that people thought that if Granny delivered a baby it was a sign of good luck. But what if everyone saw such a deformed, ugly baby and started thinking Granny had something to do with it, that it was *bad* luck for her to be around when a baby was born? What if her neighbors had started thinking the devil was even in her, thought she had 'touched' the baby in some way?"

"You could be right," Dan agreed, nodding his head. "Even if you have been away in the big city for many years now, you still have a good idea how these people around there think. Years ago it was even worse."

"So, you think she wanted the first one to die, hoping the second one would be all right?"

"I picture Granny bringing the second child, the *twin* out of Mrs. Ledbetter. When this child, Otis, looked normal, I'm sure Granny ministered to it as she should have any child. She did what was proper. However, there could be another way it went," Dan ventured.

"Such as?" Colton asked.

"Well, Ogden was probably there, saw the first baby born as did Mr. Ledbetter. Evidently, Mr. Ledbetter walked out of the room, thinking there was only the one baby. The deformity of it put him over the edge and he killed himself. We know he was mentally and emotionally unstable. That much we've learned from some of the older people around here. Well, why couldn't Ogden have gone for a doctor, the police, or some sort of help at that point? When he got back, maybe Granny told him the first baby had died and she would bury it later. He would have believed her, especially if he loved her, as you think. I like that idea, by the way. The more I think about it, I think it's an excellent theory." It was Dan's turn to pause. "Twins! Twins!" he repeated, striking the arm of the chair with his fist. "I should have seen that back at the beginning. I should have been able to put two and two together and get four. Why didn't I see that back when I first searched the Ledbetter house? Remember, I told you I ran across that old trunk in the shed with two of everything. Old things. There were two little gowns, two little pairs of bootees, even two teddy bears just alike. I didn't even think anything about the one teddy bear being well worn and the other being brand new. Hell, the price tag was still on it, around its neck. Why didn't I see it?"

"Don't blame yourself," Colton said. "How could you have known there had been twins born to Mrs. Ledbetter? If nobody else in town knew, you certainly could not have."

"Besides," Marsha added, "there's really nothing all that strange about a mother buying two of something, especially when things are on sale. I've even bought two of something for Abigail through the years, especially if it were a two-for-one sale. You can't blame yourself for anything that happened here."

"But poor Otis. Look what I put him through by arresting him for these kidnappings. Kidnappings. That's putting it mildly, isn't it?"

Colton and Marsha could see that Dan was not going to forgive himself for a while but they hated to see him beating himself up like this. The three of them had become close friends through this whole ordeal.

"Poor Otis has probably already forgotten all about it," Colton said. "I was out there the other day. He just sat calmly petting his rabbits. I had on my casual clothes. My presence didn't bother him."

They sat quietly for a few minutes. The conversation once again returned to the recent events. They would probably be talking about this, off and on, for quite a while.

"Why didn't Ledbetter wait to see what the other baby looked like?" Marsha asked.

"He probably didn't know there was another baby. Even if he did know his wife was expecting twins, maybe he thought the other one was going to come out looking just like this first one. One was enough to put him over the edge. The thought of another was absolutely unbearable to him," Colton speculated.

"Why do you think Granny kept it?" Marsha asked.

"I don't think she meant to, at first, that is," Dan replied. "Ogden did say, in his ramblings, that she was going to take it and bury it. She was not going to tell anyone about it and made him promise never to tell, either. I think, and you understand that this is all speculation on my part, that when she had delivered Otis, then went to get the other one, she expected to find it dead. When it was still alive, she just couldn't bear to kill it. After all, that would make her a murderess, even if the poor thing was horribly deformed. Another explanation was that she had just witnessed Ledbetter killing himself and she was not quite herself at that point. Maybe she thought she could take it home and love it and everything would be all right. Maybe she thought it would outgrow its deformity and ugliness. Who knows really? We only know she must have taken the baby home, kept it hidden in the basement and slowly but surely filled its subnormal mind with all kinds of insidious thought and longings. She was probably glad it was mute, like Otis."

Marsha shuddered. "But to just up and leave it boarded up in the basement, alive? How could she after she had nursed it and fed it all those years? How many years was that, anyway?"

"As best we could figure, she left it alone when it was ten years old, or about there," Dan said. "But he knew enough to survive. She had only locked the trap door in the porch with a padlock. He was so strong by that time, it didn't take him long to get through that."

They both remembered long, strong elongated arms that ended in huge, oversized hands. Those arms and legs were strong enough to break through a lock—or snap a child's neck.

"Yeah, that well-hidden trap door in the floor of the side porch," Dan added. I bet no one ever went around that way, since you had to go around that old swing at the corner of the porch that was still hanging by one chain from the ceiling by the time we saw it. What a perfect place for a hidden door. I can see how searchers at various times through the years overlooked it."

"But why do you think she left the…child?…after all that time?" Marsha insisted.

Colton shrugged. "Well, again, I can only offer my opinion, but I think just the knowledge of what she had done, the knowledge of its very existence, drove her more and more insane. She really began to think of it as an evil thing. Her mind probably went back to the idea of a baby like that being of the devil. She could have gotten her idea of evil from that. The idea probably just kept growing and growing inside her, eating away at her sanity. That and guilt, of course. Who knows, really?"

"Yeah," Dan agreed. "I'm not sure it was evil of itself. I think it just didn't know what to do after Granny left, and there was no one to bring it food. And she had given it no morals. Either that or the problem was that she tried to teach it things, and it simply could not comprehend what she tried to teach it. She was probably afraid to kill it, in case someone found the body. Then how to explain anything? So she insisted the family move after they boarded up the basement. She was hoping it would starve to death. All creatures have an instinct for self-survival, and the first thought it had was probably of food. It had to eat," he said. He was not justifying its actions, simply stating a fact.

"Yeah, it had to eat, all right," Colton agreed.

The End

About the Author

Mary Jane Bryan is a graduate of Missouri State University (SEMO), Cape Girardeau, Missouri, with a BS in Business Administration/General Management and a graduate of Three Rivers Community College, Poplar Bluff, Missouri, with an AA in General Studies.

Bryan is strong believer in women as entrepreneurs and managers, and she is a past creator and owner of Jane's Muppets. She is a past member of Toastmasters International, which is an excellent resource for creative writing and presentation, receiving critiques and advice as needed. A past resident of Ecuador, Bryan now currently resides in Farmington, Missouri, with her husband, Peter, and their cat, Cookie.